The Snow Angel

Jayne Fresina

A TWISTED E PUBLISHING BOOK

The Snow Angel
Copyright © 2018 by Jayne Fresina

Edited by Marie Medina

Cover design by K Designs
All cover art and logo copyright © 2018, Twisted E-Publishing, LLC

ALL RIGHTS RESERVED: This literary work may not be reproduced or transmitted in any form or by any means, including electronic or photographic reproduction, in whole or in part, without express written permission.

All characters and events in this book are fictitious. Any resemblance to actual persons living or dead is strictly coincidental.

ISBN: 9781790119110

It's Christmas 1877 and Anne Follyot— of little beauty and no fortune, but sturdy spirit and an excess of imagination— is invited to stay with her favorite aunt in Cornwall. She's all anticipation, waiting for the man chosen to escort her on this journey. According to her aunt, she met him before, many years ago, but Anne cannot remember him and she's positive that he must long-since have forgotten her. She's never been memorable.

But J.P. Deverell, Esq. is now a grown man with a dangerous reputation, of which her aunt cannot possibly be aware. And Anne means to make the most of her aunt's mistake and this adventure. She considers herself a modern, independent woman, for whom a little scandal is well overdue. If she doesn't seize this chance now, she might never have another.

As Charles Dickens wrote, "No space of regret can make amends for one life's opportunity misused."

* * * *

He's in no temper for eggnog and mistletoe; no mood to tolerate the painfully polite company of some plain spinster, in a carriage, for three days. It's probably a contrivance to get him home for Christmas.

Remember Anne Follyot? He doesn't care to remember *himself* sixteen years ago, let alone recall the dull vicar's five year-old niece.

He'd planned to spend his Yuletide working, alone and in peace. But a letter from his mother has guilted him into this act of begrudging chivalry, aided by the whispers of his best friend's mischievous ghost.

"Bah, Humbug!" As Charles Dickens also wrote.

* * * *

But this journey will not turn out quite the way either traveler expects, for when these two opposites collide, so do ghosts of the past, the present and the future.

It will be a holiday season with all the usual fare—peril, pandemonium, family quarrels, mulled wine and bodily injury. Certainly a Christmas adventure never to be forgotten this time.

At least, by one of them.

Chapter One
December 20th, 1877

The teller of this tale must hereby begin with an apology, for undoubtedly our leading man is not, at first chapter, the stuff of which romantic heroes are made. Except, perhaps, for the brooding, constipated expression into which his features most naturally fall, quite unintentionally possessing an air of thwarted passion and wounded bear.

But since he read few novels himself, he could have no idea of the stormy, ardent imaginings that his menacing frown inspired in the minds and hearts of the hapless young women he passed— readers and devourers of Brontë, Gaskell and Austen. He simply thought them all tied too tightly into their corsets and hairpins, or that their glacé kid shoes were new and pinched. Apart from that he paid little attention to their antics. Females were, in general, hysterical creatures; it was well documented. As engines ran on coal and steam, woman ran on smelling salts, screaming fits and accusations.

He did not intend to commence the cost of keeping one himself on a permanent arrangement at any time in the near future.

As in the case of most folk, he was in such haste to get where he was going that day— which was a Thursday, not that it matters much, but he likes to be particular–– that he very nearly missed the journey completely and, consequently, could have missed *her* too. But on this day an angel, not taking any chances, came along and knocked seven bells out of him.

Angels, he was about to learn, can do that to a man; they are not the dainty, ethereal creatures one might imagine.

So at least you know he will get his comeuppance, even if you do not like him much yet. Let that be the salve for your disappointment in finding him fall so far short in all the necessary accoutrements of the knight in shining armor.

Before *she* walked into his life, he was a man who thought he could plan and structure an orderly route through his life; that he was in charge of his own destiny; that he knew everything, wanted for nothing. Even his stride was confident, forceful, changing course for nobody, as if the pavement was privileged to exist under his boots, and everybody who strolled upon it owed him a debt of gratitude for enriching the air with his presence.

Commandeering the street in his usual fashion, his forward motion pausing or diverting for nobody, he sailed along on that Thursday with incautious speed. His fiercely scowling brows, like the wings of a giant hawk poised for flight above the raised high collar of his greatcoat, caused anxious folk to clutch their small children aside, but still he paid no heed to anything directly under his feet.

Which is how it happened that he tumbled.

One moment, his grim perusal— filled with the reflection of snow-laden clouds— was fixed on a distant point, far away in his thoughts; in the next he was felled to his knees from that great and lofty height, like the wooden dummy in a game of Aunt Sally. And because he was unaccustomed to the sudden loss of power over his own limbs, the fall was even more awkward, ungainly and— such is human nature—comical to those who watched.

A gloved hand reached down, fingers grasping his coat sleeve.

"Steady there, young man," a husky voice exclaimed, half-laughing. "Look where you're going, before 'tis too late."

In that moment, no more than the blink of an eye, he thought he saw white feathers.

Flushed and hot, aware of folk turning to stare and chuckle, he straightened up in haste and pulled his arm away from the old woman's grip. "Thank you," he muttered, angrily brushing down his coat sleeves and glaring at the dent he'd left in the abandoned trunk at his feet. "I am quite alright."

"Are you? Keep your eyes open, sir, or you will look back one day and wonder where all the time went. Enjoy every breath and don't waste it cursing at the weather. Such things a man cannot change for the better. Some things he can."

He felt foolish enough, falling in the street, without being lectured to in this odd fashion by a stranger. And a woman, at that! The London streets were full of pickpockets and chancers, so he was always guarded and wary, especially around those with an overly-familiar manner. "Yes...well...good day. Get out of my way then." He stepped around the trunk, trying to ignore the pain in his knee.

See me.

After a few yards, certain the whispering old woman followed him very closely— walking in his very footsteps— he turned his head to demand her purpose.

See me.

But she was nowhere in sight, disappearing into the festive, milling crowd.

"Hot chestnuts!" A man with a cart barked from the corner, filling paper cones with his wares. "Git yer hot chestnuts here for ha'penny!"

The snow that had threatened all afternoon finally began to fall. Ah, that must be what he saw, when he thought there were feathers on the old lady's shoulder— the first snowflakes.

Scowling, he dug his chin deeper into the coils of woolen scarf inside his collar and limped onward. Into the softly falling snow and, by averting his course, into our story.

* * * *

December, 1927

Where had all the time between gone?

Ironically, as a young scrapper he'd felt wise beyond his years, all-knowing; now, as an old man he was humbled, aware of just how much he did not know and never would; of how much would always remain a mystery.

If a chap looked back at his life too often, so he'd found, he could get lost in it and forget to move forward. So for that reason he did not reminisce about the past, if it could be avoided. He did not want to be caught napping and run over by his limber, youthful, arrogant, un-creaky self.But Christmas was the worst of times for such pondering. All that eggnog and sentiment fogged the mind and tempted him to think back over the years and remember. Sometimes with an unmanly tear in his eye.

Anybody who knew him very well would never dare attempt to poke that tear out of him or to mention having seen it, for he could still be exceedingly thorny and cantankerous under those circumstances, as he liked to warn folk.

"Only under those circumstances?" his saucy grand-daughter had once remarked.

"I am entitled, at the age of eighty, to be disagreeable and contrary. I've earned the right. And there will be no more opportunity once I'm in my grave and quiet, so I shall make the most of it while I can."

"Oh," she had replied drily, "shall you be quiet in your grave? I should imagine you'll find a dozen ways to come back and haunt us all. I've never known you sit still for more than a quarter of an hour, and once you're a spirit free to ramble, unhindered by the limitations of the flesh, I'm sure there will be no peace for anybody. Besides you may be eighty, but I've taught eight year-olds in my class at school who are better behaved."

Eight years old. He once claimed those few years himself, of course, writing it boldly and proudly inside the cover of his school books.

Property of J. P. Deverell, 8 yeres. This be his book. Do not theefe or he will strike ye about that thick head and poke out ye eyes with thawny sticke.

He smiled, thinking of it now. All that time ago and yet it could be yesterday.

As a young boy he'd often felt like a somber old man, never quite on a level footing with others his age. But the more tired and worn his bones became, the younger and more inquisitive the spirit caged within them. He supposed that was why the soul eventually had to be set free, once it no longer had need of the body to protect it from the elements—when that cage was merely a hindrance, holding it back. In the beginning, of course, the being within needed the shield of flesh and bone to traverse the adventure of life, so that when it tumbled and was knocked about only the scaffold was damaged.

Well, that was his theory.

Hers too. Hers first probably.

Tonight, as he looked out on the stars and moon of a crisp winter's eve, memories pulled at him like the cold hands of a beggar child, impossible to ignore.

Because fifty Christmases ago his life changed forever. Fifty, it seemed such an impossible number of years gone by. A large number and yet so small in many ways.

He looked around at the walls of his granddaughter's house and found that he saw everything with brighter eyes tonight, as if he was that young man again. Oh, if only he had known then all that he knew now. Or even as much as he thought he knew. But, as the saying went, youth was wasted on the young.

Even the poppies and cornflowers on the wallpaper took on new luster this evening, as if he could reach out and pluck them with his hand. The holly on the mantle shone with brilliant, plump, scarlet berries and lush, rustling, emerald leaves, and in among them the precious pearls of mistletoe nestled, waiting to be held aloft by kissing couples. Downstairs, on the wireless, a distant choir sang. Astonishing that such miracles could be produced, he thought— voices captured through the air. When he was a young boy of eight such a thing might as well be witchcraft.

The air was warm and spiced with the scents of Christmas, a heady combination of cinnamon, nutmeg and almonds, of brandy-soaked raisins and melt-in-the-mouth mince pies. Of anticipation, wistfulness and hope. Of magic.

There was a time when he did not appreciate all this. He was in too much haste.

Now his eyes were open.

At his side a little girl, with a great many years yet ahead of her, looked up at him and demanded, "Tell me a story!" Drowsy but still defiant, she pleaded. "Please, tell me one of your stories, Jeepers."

But he'd been in trouble before with his granddaughter for telling tales she considered too gory or frightening for her eight-year-old. "That imagination of yours gets worse," she had exclaimed earlier that day, getting in a huff over the Christmas pudding when he interrupted her stirring to dip a finger into the mixture. "Why can't you tell her a nice, happy-ever-after fairy tale for once? Honestly, the things that girl comes out with and she gets it all from you!"

"A fairy tale? Not all fairies are good, you know. Some are downright wicked."

"You know what I mean, grandpapa."

"An unlikely tale in which romance blossoms out of the cinders and everybody lives happily after?" He had shaken his head, lips pursed. "What good does it do to fill a young girl's mind with that nonsense? I'm surprised at you. Ten years ago you and your mother were marching for the vote."

"Lizzie is eight, grandfather. Let her have her fairy tales a while longer. She should not hear of bloody bones, severed heads and vampires at her age."

So he had walked out of her kitchen, advising sulkily, "Damn pudding needs more brandy. If you're going to do a job you ought to do it properly."

No, he was not very good with fairy tales and his great grand-daughter didn't like them anyway.

She yawned, stretching and nestling into his shoulder, just like a cat. "You tell the best stories, Jeepers."

He took the half empty cup of Ovaltine from her hands, before she spilled it. "Perhaps I can read to you about the lives of real women who do important things. Your mother ought to approve of that, surely." Fumbling for a pile of books on the shelf beside her bed, he squinted through his spectacles at the titles. "What have we here? Florence Nightingale. Emmeline Pankhurst. Marie Curie—"

"Not tonight," she groaned impatiently. "It's Christmas. Tell me another story. A good one."

"You've heard them all. Does this old, grey head look as if it keeps so much stored inside? Most of what was once there has long-since leaked out through these holes on the side of my head. See them?" He pointed to his ears.

"Then make up a new one."

"I'm not Charles Dickens, young lady."

"But it's Christmas."

"And that's an excuse for you to get everything your way, is it?" he grumbled, putting the books back on the shelf and taking off his spectacles. "Well, I can't—"

There, among the little girl's favored possessions, sat a wooden box with brass hinges and an ivory inlaid pattern of snowdrops across the lid.

He paused, closed his eyes.

"Jeepers? Are you falling asleep?"

The breath swelled in his chest and he was a boy again, surrounded by flickering candles, sparks that shimmered, and the warm, spicy scent of oranges, cloves and pine boughs. He saw his own fingers, quick, agile, self-assured and entirely painless again— a state he'd almost forgotten they'd ever known— folding paper. Yes, white paper. A girl's face looked up, watching him in wonder. For just a moment she was there, but too soon gone as he tried to grasp the detail. Like a snowflake on a boy's hot fingertip, she melted.

"Asleep?" He opened his eyes, frustrated. "I most certainly am not asleep, missy!" With a slightly trembling hand, he lifted the wooden box down and set it on the blanket before her. "As a matter of fact, I do know one more story that I haven't told you yet."

She clasped her hands together under her chin. "Good."

"It all happened a long time ago, of course."

"These things generally do," she agreed somberly.

"Long before there were songs on the wireless, Ovaltine, or electric Christmas tree lights."

Slowly he opened the lid of the box and up popped a little figure in a white silk and tulle frock with goose feather wings and a halo of glass beads— some clear, some opaque and some painted silver, so that they glistened just like frost on a snowy bough. When carefully wound up, she turned and fluttered her wings to the tune of The Wexford Carol. A favorite song of his. And of hers. Of hers first probably.

So much of hers had become his over the years: likes and dislikes, favorite songs and stories. Memories. He must have been empty before *she* came along.

"That's my snow angel," said his great granddaughter.

"I know. I never told you how she came to live here in this box, did I?"

"No," she whispered, as if the angel might be listening. Peering up at his face, studying his expression, she added, "Is it a sad story, Jeepers? Or a ghost story? Or a love story?"

"A little bit of all that. 'Tis a tale I've never told to another person in all my one hundred and eighty years. Only you."

Her lips parted to exhale a gasp of sleepy excitement.

He looked out at the stars through her snow-spattered bedroom window. "I suppose it's time I told you and then you can carry it on, so that when I'm gone it is not forgotten. Stories are like hearts, you see. They cannot live on alone, kept selfishly to one's self. They have to be shared."

She wriggled to get more comfortable, settling in against his shoulder, listening to the gentle music and watching the snow angel's slow, glittering pirouettes. "Proceed," she said grandly, "I am ready."

"Well, then." He straightened a feather on the snow angel's wing. "It began," he said, "on a night much like this one, but many, many years ago."

"Was it snowing?"

"Oh, yes. It had just begun to snow and a young man— well, not quite that young perhaps in years, but still younger than he thought he was at the time— a man, who—"

"Was he handsome?"

"Not at all."

"He wasn't a prince?"

"Princes are not always handsome, you know. Many a toad is more appealing to the eye. And they eat insects, a valuable service. Also, they swallow with their eyeballs, so a certain lady once told me."

She looked up at him skeptically. "The hero of your story is a toad?"

"You won't find out unless you cease jabbering, miss. Well, then. This exceedingly unhandsome, youngish fellow was about to embark upon an extraordinary journey. Not that he knew it yet. He had no knowledge of what lay in store. While he thought he knew everything, of course, he knew nothing." He reached up and dimmed the gas lamp on the wall above the bed.

"But strange, wonderful and miraculous things can happen this time of year, even to a man who is jaded and stubborn and not in the least bit deserving of them. Even a man who did not believe in the magic of Christmas.

In fact, he had been heard to say..."

Chapter Two
London, December 1877

"Bah Humbug! I quite agree with Ebenezer Scrooge. There, I've said it. And shall do so again. *Bah*, and furthermore, *Humbug*." Having made his point and fixed it with a swig of brandy, John Paul Deverell slouched deeper into his dimpled leather chair and exhaled a most impolite burp. A noise to which— as he would have pointed out had anybody dared reprimand him— he was entitled, in his own office, on his own time and with, blessedly, no females present. "If you ask me, Ebenezer Scrooge is a character greatly maligned and misunderstood."

"Like you, sir?" ventured his clerk with only a very slight lift of one eyebrow.

"Precisely. Why the poor man should be obliged to change everything in his life and his character just to please a few self-righteous, hypocritical wretches and Christmas Carol caterwaulers, I'll never know. Is a man who makes his own fortune in life no longer entitled to do with it as he pleases? Is he to apologize for saving his pennies and shillings rather than throwing them about like bird seed or handing them off to every gin-swilling vagrant in the street? No problem was ever solved by throwing money at it, Shepherd. Ask my father. That was how he dealt with his children, and they all turned out spoiled, self-indulgent and stupid."

"Except for you, sir. Of course," came the reply. "You are the very epitome of restraint and wisdom. And stringent accounting."

He waved his empty brandy snifter in casual dismissal of this wry flattery. "Well it was different for me. By the time I came along, my father was considerably older and wiser."

"Usually, sir, the youngest in a family is everybody's pet."

"*Pet?*" He sat up, almost getting out of the chair, until he remembered his sore knee and then fell back, wincing. "I can assure you I was never any such thing."

"Merely an observation on the customary consequence, sir, of being the last born," said the clerk hurriedly, as he finished wrapping a woolen scarf around his neck. Ducking his head to peer out of the window at the first flakes of snow, he added, "Looks as if I'd best make haste and get home then, sir, if you've naught else tonight."

"Yes." Deverell sighed. "You'd better go home to your loved ones."

The clerk hesitated. "You have no company this evening, sir?"

"No, and glad I am of it."

"Seems a shame for a you to be on your own, abandoned and limping around. And with Christmas coming."

"*Abandoned?* Suits me. Ah, to be left alone and in peace. That is the very thing I would consider a Christmas gift."

"You don't mean that, sir. Nobody should be alone this time of year."

"Do stop hovering over me, man! You have three miles to walk home, after all."

"Oh, I shall catch the omnibus tonight, sir."

"The omnibus?" he muttered, shaking his head. "Such an expense on a clerk's salary? Even that of a head clerk?"

Shepherd ventured a bit of smile. "It is Christmas, sir, and snowing. I think my purse will stretch to the hedonistic luxury of a seat on the omnibus this once. You pay me a generous wage, sir. Although I know you don't care to be reminded of it."

He rolled his eyes. "Christmas," he said flatly. "How did it happen that Christmas stretched to include an entire week, when once it was merely a single day of inconvenience?"

"It was your insistence that I take five days off, sir."

"But the omnibus too?"

"I've packages to carry, sir. The brandy you gave me and gifts for the wife and children."

"Mind yourself, Shepherd. 'Tis a slippery slope upon which you embark with this riotous merriment. Two good stout walks daily keep a man fit and in health. Once you start taking the omnibus, willy-nilly, it will become a regular occurrence. You will find yourself tempted to sit down a great deal more than is good for anybody and then poor Mrs. Shepherd—who I'm sure has much to do already keeping that cottage, which you purchased for such a ridiculously inflated price, quite clean and tidy, not to mention those children you thoughtlessly sprang upon her—will have the additional trouble of letting out all your clothes."

"Your concern for Mrs. Shepherd is most kindly, sir, and I shall be sure and tell her that you wish her a merry Christmas, shall I?"

"You will do nothing of the sort. I would not want to rub salt in the wound of her misfortune, by suggesting that this miserably cold season, stuck at home with you and those wild offspring for five whole days, could be anything for her other than hard labor." He shook his head. "Well, I tried to warn her, but she would have none of it. Somehow you talked her into marriage and she, in common with most females, could not be set right with a dosing of common sense. She made her bed and now,"— he shook his head, grim— "she must lie in it."

The clerk laughed, unable to hold it in this time.

"I see the so-called '*spirit of the season*' makes you senseless and giddy, Shepherd. Go on, off with you. I shall expect you here promptly at eight o' the clock next Wednesday morning, mind, ready to work. However much you might have overindulged during this wretched bacchanalia."

"Five days, sir," exclaimed Shepherd, rubbing his gloved hands gleefully together. "Are you sure I can have five entire days off? Perhaps you misspoke on a whim and now wish you had my company for the season."

"A *whim*? Since when have you known me do anything on a whim?"

"Well, you did change barbers last week. For the first time in twelve years."

"Because old Johnson's rheumatics do not allow him to hold a razor without endangering life and limb anymore, I was obliged to seek a new barber. It was not by choice and certainly not by whim. Don't press your luck, Shepherd, or I might yet change my mind about these five days you winkled out of me."

"It does seem excessive, sir, especially with the shop so busy and I let several of the young ladies take time away with their families already, as I did not know you would offer the holiday to me."

"For pity's sake, I believe we can hold down the fort in your absence without burning the place to the ground. Besides, Parslow, of the shiny, scrubbed face, was eager to step into your shoes for a week. We shall see how he does with the added responsibility. I daresay the experience will cause him to regard you with new respect and take some of the shine off his damnably rosy cheeks. Serves him right. No man should be that happy all the time."

His clerk laughed again and was almost through the door when he stopped abruptly and turned ashen above the folds of his scarf so that it looked as if that woolen snake really did crush the breath out of him, ready to swallow his bones. "Oh, crikey, sir! I very nearly forgot! A letter arrived for you just this afternoon while you were out. With all the commotion over your nasty fall on Bond Street, sir—", he gestured at the bandaged knee and the makeshift walking cane by his employer's chair, "—I set it aside. Then, after your generous offer of brandy and mince pie, well...it escaped my mind until this very minute." Hastily dashing behind a desk in the corner, he sorted through the pile of paper and retrieved a sealed missive. "I daresay it was held up with bad weather, sir, for according to the mark it was sent some time since."

"Then I hope you did not see fit to pay the boy extra for delivery."

"It is almost Christmas, sir, and he was fully contrite about the delay."

Deverell groaned and held out his hand. "For the love of scrumpy, I am clearly in the wrong profession. Nobody ever seeks to pay me extra to fail at my job. Frequently they complain about rising prices and being presented with any bill at all for our wares, as if *'on account'* should mean for eternity and we ought to work for charity. Meanwhile, here I am soldered to my desk over the season, while everybody else dashes home, on the omnibus, to a motley crowd of loved ones. I receive no thanks. Not a whimper."

"The staff are accustomed to you working up here all hours, sir. They think nothing of it. They don't know that you have any life away from the office, sir. They've never seen your face emerge from it. And since Mr. Dockery passed on in such an untimely manner— God rest his soul— you work even more than you ever did. You're always here. When a man never spares time for himself, other folk take advantage, sir."

Grumbling under his breath about the inconvenience caused by his business partner's thoughtlessness in dying suddenly, Deverell set his empty glass down and tore open the letter. Wherever it had been on its journey to get there, it looked as if a litter of riotous piglets had made it their plaything.

At once he recognized his mother's handwriting and knew that she had written urging him home to Roscarrock Castle for Christmas. She had no appreciation for the demands of his work and thought he could simply drop everything to travel three long days— six, when one accounted for the return trip— to spend less than a handful of hours between in feigned jollity with half-siblings who neither knew nor cared about his life. Indeed, he was certain they barely knew that he was in the room unless they felt a draft.

"You might at least come home and visit once a year, J.P. One never knows when it might be your dear old father's last Christmas."

Last Christmas, indeed. His "dear old" father was the sprightliest, most irritatingly healthy septuagenarian in England. Possibly the world. Not that anybody knew for sure his age, not even the man himself— or so he claimed. And when his mother pulled out that particular weapon with which to assault their son's conscience, she did so with a considerable amount of tongue in cheek.

This year, however, there was something new added to the usual hints about his dereliction of sonly duty.

"I must beg a favor of you, my darling J.P.
My old friend and former neighbor, the widowed Mrs. Follyot, expects a visit from her husband's niece; a poor, sickly creature who is obliged to travel for urgent reasons, despite her weak health. Rather than see the young lady exposed to the undignified, unreliable horrors of a public coach, or the peril of railway travel— which, despite your father's assurances, I firmly refuse to countenance for anybody I care the slightest about—I suggested you might be amenable to the idea of escorting her as far as Widecombe in your own carriage. I thought it would be a good deed you might dispatch with limited hardship to yourself, while on your way home to us. I hear you bought a fine carriage recently, which you have not yet used to visit us at Roscarrock, and it will hardly put you out to escort one timid young lady in it. She is not likely to be any trouble and, I thought, will be less weight for your springs than is produced by that hefty scowl falling upon your face as you read this..."

Despite his mother's cheerful use of "suggested", "might", and "thought", she went on to write,

"So I took the liberty of assuring Mrs. Follyot that her niece will be safe in your hands and she writes to her directly. Miss Anne Follyot, will, therefore, anticipate your arrival at the enclosed address at five o' the clock on the evening of Thursday the 20th. That is the earliest she can escape her duties in Town. I hope the roads will be largely emptied by then and you should be with us to dine on Christmas Eve, if not sooner.

Do be gentle with the poor girl."

Furious, he consulted his fob watch. It was a quarter to five.

He certainly had good reason to say it was too late for anything to be done. However, his mother had sent the letter more than a week ago and it was not her fault, he supposed reluctantly, that it arrived on that very day of the 20th. Damn and blast.

It was also not her fault that he'd tripped over some careless wretch's trunk in the icy street and twisted his knee that afternoon.

"Although it is not entirely proper and eyebrows might be raised, my friend agrees that the urgency of the circumstance— and the young lady's frailty—makes for an exception. Besides, the two of you have met once before, Mrs. Follyot assures me, when her husband was the vicar of Porthwellen. There was a vicarage tea party for the village children some sixteen or seventeen years ago. Perhaps you will remember little Anne?"

Remember Anne? He did not care to remember himself sixteen years ago, let alone some feeble girl he'd supposedly met once.

"Looks as if you'll be going home for Christmas, after all, sir," said Shepherd, cheekily reading over his shoulder. "You can recover there from your fall, with loving family to look after you. 'Tis splendid news."

J.P. clutched the letter to his chest, away from those prying, impertinent eyes. "Is it? I see no cause for such good cheer."

"But now I needn't worry about you being here all alone and grim for the Yuletide. That's a relief, so it is."

"At least one of us is happy then."

"In actual fact, sir, it is lucky you took your fall when you did, or you would not have come back here to the office this afternoon, I would have gone home by now, and that letter would have been forgotten on my desk until next Wednesday."

J.P. had been on his way to an assignation in Kensington that afternoon, but after he was attacked by that stray trunk and put into such a foul mood, he decided to limp back to his office instead. Then his knee really began to throb and thus, feeling sorry for himself, he'd flopped back into his chair and reached for the brandy. All thoughts of traversing the dangerous curves of Mrs. Marvington in her hotel suite, even for an hour, were soon brushed aside.

The lady would find other company, no doubt. For a scandalous divorcee she had a very full social calendar, although she claimed J.P. was her only lover.

He forced his attention back to the head clerk, who was saying, "Mrs. Shepherd would have fretted all season, to think of you suffering and not able to get about after your fall, sir."

He pushed himself up higher in the chair. "Shepherd, kindly stop referring to the incident as *'Your Fall'* in that manner. It makes me sound like an ancient and infirm fellow for whom a tumble was inevitable. A rite of passage, like a broken hip, a receding hairline and gout. At thirty I may no longer lay claim to youthful folly, but I am not yet fit for a bath-chair."

Shepherd laughed. "Sometimes I forget you're only thirty. I can't imagine why. Goodnight to you then, sir, and all the best for the season. I know you say you don't believe in it, but you'll have a merry Christmas in any case, whether you want it or not. You deserve it, sir, and I've got a feeling about it this year. I'll let Jarvis know you do need the carriage after all." As the clerk left the office, his jaunty whistle echoed around the walls, further deepening J.P.'s new headache.

Christmas. Bah, humbug.

His mother, he was convinced, had concocted this nonsense as a way to make him go home. Did she think her son addled that he could not see through the deception? Well, she could—

A sudden draft extinguished two candles on his desk. Must have been Shepherd closing and locking the front door of the shop downstairs. Wind guttered down the chimney, bringing with it a smattering of icy glitter, a brisk reminder of the weather outside.

Abruptly he envisioned a wilting creature waiting across town in the snow, clutching a tattered carpet bag, her last feverish breaths exhaled through blue lips in a wail of despair. The London streets, as darkness fell, were no place for a woman alone and apparently she had no one else since she must resort to calling upon *his* services in this matter.

Perhaps you remember little Anne?

No. Not a wisp of hair on her frail and dainty head.

"You know you cannot leave her there," a voice whispered in his ear, brought, it seemed, by the draft.

He turned his head. "Dockery? Is that you?"

But how could it be? Jacob Dockery, his best friend since their school days together, was dead, struck down without warning last Christmas. A thin vessel in his brain had broken, just like that, and he was gone, snapped away like a twig in the winter wind. All these years the tiny thing that would be his end had lurked there in secret, waiting for its moment, ticking away inside his dear friend.

"We never know how long we've got, and I know that better than anybody now," the voice murmured softly. "You must make the most of your time. Don't sit here alone. You've things to do. Life to live, love to give."

Yes, it sounded like Dockery; it was the sort of thing that optimistic fool was known to utter. Especially when he'd drunk too much.

"I *am* living life," J.P. replied, terse. "I work every hour to keep Lockreedy and Velder on its feet. Since you left me all alone to carry on, what choice do I have?"

"You haven't had a day off in a year."

"I must keep an eye on the place."

"And nobody sits at my desk to help you."

"I have Shepherd."

"But he is most often down on the shop floor. Why not give him a promotion and my desk? You cannot bear the weight entirely upon your own shoulders. You should not."

Deverell looked over at his old friend's deserted corner, where he could not bear to see another soul seated. Not yet. "One day your son will take over your desk," he muttered crossly. "I hold the position for him."

"Little Charles may be something of a genius— unlike his dear departed papa— but it will be a great while yet before the boy can take up that chair." His friend laughed softly. "He is but three years of age and already owes much to you."

"He owes me naught. I would never see him or his mother suffer."

"Yet you did not think me right to marry when I did four years ago."

"Knowing your wandering eye, I thought the matter imprudent and the woman perhaps not in full possession of her wits to accept you, but it was done and when milk is spilled one does not waste time and energy lamenting over the stain."

He could hardly have left the young Mrs. Dockery abandoned when his friend died so suddenly. She had quarreled with her wealthy, stern father, who disliked Jacob and refused to sanction the match or to recognize his daughter after the wedding. Four years later, with her young husband dead, a little son by her side and another child on the way, she'd had nobody else in London to help her, except J.P.

"I made certain she is provided for. She and the children will want for nothing that is within reason."

"But now what of you, my friend?" whispered Jacob. "Who will tend your needs and provide for you?"

"I provide for myself. And why the devil are you down here haunting me tonight? Is the party up there so very dull?" He had every confidence that there would be a party. If there had not been any festivities in progress already when Jacob got there, he would have organized some immediately.

"Because you need me to show you that you're stuck in the wheel ruts, old chap. You must *heave-ho* and roll forward. You must keep moving with life. Don't get left behind. I'm here to prod you until you move. I shall use the carrot or the stick. Whichever works, you sizeable, irascible ass. And you're right— I am missing the party, so make haste."

"My knee hurts too much to move, thanks to whomever left their damnable trunk in the street today."

"It cannot hurt that badly. I've seen you throw bigger men than yourself to the ground on a muddy university rugby field and then been landed upon yourself with nothing more than a slight wince to your expression. Another glass of brandy will help. Come on, J.P., put on your hat and coat and do a good deed."

"Why?" he grumbled. "When was the last time anybody did a good deed for me?"

His friend laughed. "Perhaps this is it. Shepherd said he has a feeling about it."

He shook his head and glowered at the smoldering coals in the grate. Bob Shepherd's "feelings" had been a matter of great amusement to Jacob.

"What's your feeling, Shepherd, about the Epsom Derby this year?" he would exclaim.

"My money's on Kisber, sir." came the confident reply.

On another day, it was, "*How many customers will walk through our door today, Shepherd? What's your feeling in that case?*"

"Eighty, sir."
"I shall say seventy. And will it rain all day?"
"Only until noon, sir."
"I shall say one."

They frequently passed their days in this fashion, wagering on everything and anything, just between themselves and seldom for anything more than a penny. Jacob loved to gamble, and it both fascinated and annoyed him that the head clerk could be right so often, plucking names and numbers out of the air with scarcely a thought.

"*I do not know why you continue the stupidity*," J.P. had said to his friend more than once.

"*Because on the few occasions I win, it is an enormous thrill.*"

It had never occurred to Jacob, apparently, that Shepherd deliberately let him win, once in a while, simply to keep him playing. By the time Jacob died, the head clerk had very probably amassed a small fortune from their little game as all those pennies added up.

No wonder he could afford the omnibus.

"I shan't go away, old chap," said the voice in the draft again, "until you agree to go out into the snow and fetch that poor invalid girl to her aunt. You know what an irritating pest I can be. I shall make you leave that chair just to get away from me. Now, what shall I sing to cheer your spirits?"

"No singing!"

Laughing, his old friend defied him, of course, and took up where Shepherd's whistling had faded away. Soon the wretched Good King Wenceslas was haunting J.P., over and over again, looking out at deep and crisp and even snow on the Feast of Stephen, like an automaton with an over-wound clockwork and a loose spring.

The term, "No peace for the wicked" came to his mind.

A conscience, as he'd always suspected, was a terrible, inconvenient thing. Especially when it took on the voice of a dead friend. Especially at Christmas.

Chapter Three

Now to our heroine; a young woman of neither fortune nor beauty, but sturdy spirit and an excess of imagination. So often had Anne Follyot heard herself described as such, that she was certain it would be carved upon her gravestone.

Along with one other phrase, if her brother had his way.

Finally silent.

"Anne always has too much to say for herself," her brother had declared loudly just before their mother's funeral, eleven years before, "as if anybody wants to hear what she thinks about anything. Her chattering tongue shows a peculiar want of humility and is most unladylike."

This accusation came because Anne had suggested that she and her little sister might be allowed to follow the coffin and attend the funeral. But Wilfred, being six years her senior, overruled her wishes, advising their father that it would not be seemly for the girls to go along. This was, she suspected, an old-fashioned way of thinking, but Wilfred was a young man who only followed fashion when it had some benefit to himself.

"It is still not the done thing in any family of *polite* society, father," he had said. "What will folk think of us to see Anne and Lizzie grieving in public? It is an insult to decency and cannot be condoned if we are to keep proper standards of etiquette. It would be an embarrassment, father. Nobody wants to see little girls crying at a funeral."

Anne suspected her brother was afraid he might be reduced to unmanly tears himself if he heard his sisters weeping, and that would never do.

So Anne and her sister stayed at home in the care of their favorite aunt, while their brother, in great state and a very fine black hat purchased for the occasion, followed the coffin with their bereft father. They hired "mutes", of course, professional mourners to keep the grief suitably in order.

She had not thought of that day for quite some time, trying to keep her mood cheerful, but tonight, so many years later, the memory came back to her—particularly the kindness of her Aunt Follyot, who had sat reading to the girls on that rainy afternoon of their mother's funeral, a calm, sweet presence, always knowing exactly what to say and do, what was needed, never relying on fashionable society to guide her actions. Probably not having the slightest desire to know what the "upper classes" did, because she was happy and content in her own life. Something Wilfred Follyot could never be.

Poor Wilf. Nobody wanted more from the world than he did, and yet he always seemed to take the wrong steps, the wrong choices, burying himself in debt and responsibility and then blaming anything and anybody else for it.

Ten years later, at their father's funeral, Anne had determinedly stood up for herself and her sister, declaring that they were "modern girls" and would attend, whether her brother approved or not. As a result of her rebellion, when he was not pretending to snub her, Wilf had spent the entire service glowering at her from beneath his hat brim. At the graveside she'd heard him tell the curate that, "Anne has always been difficult. I do not know what will become of her now that she no longer has our father to manage. I hope she does not think to come and live with me, for I can spare no room and I dread to think of the influence she would have on my own girls. No, we must find somewhere to put Anne."

As if he hoped the curate might recommend an asylum, or a nunnery.

But her brother need not have worried, for Anne already knew what she would do next with her life, and neither his help, nor his counsel, nor his reluctant hospitality, were required.

What would he think of his irritating sister tonight— the adventure upon which she was about to embark?

Most certainly he would call this improper too. Perhaps even indecent.

Yet tonight her brother could not stop her. He no longer had that power over his sister for she had freed herself of it, taking bold steps toward independence by earning her own money. Shocking. No doubt another embarrassment for Wilf to explain to his fine friends. Although by now he had most likely ceased to talk of her at all to save himself the need for any explanation.

She shivered, half with cold, half with something else for which she had not yet invented a name, because it was an entirely new sensation.

There was quite a draft through that passage. More than a draft, actually; wind might be a more accurate term. On very cold days, frost built up inside the window and had to be scraped off with a butter knife. Tonight, the wind that whistled through the badly fitted panes seemed to be singing a tune. She had to bounce on her heels a little to keep her blood circulating and prevent it freezing solid in her veins. And since she was bouncing anyway, she decided to hum too, amusing herself by making the flame of her candle twist and dance to the rhythm of her breath.

"That Deverell still not here yet?" her landlady called out as she passed through the hall with the tea tray. "It's well after five, surely. Near six by now."

She ceased humming mid-note and put on her most sensible, patient face, carefully holding the candle away with both hands, rather than be accused of playing fast and loose with that precious commodity. "I daresay he will come when he can, Mrs. Smith. He's a busy gentleman, I understand, and it is very good of him to make room in his plans for me at all."

Mrs. Smith plainly thought the word "gentleman" unsuitable in this case, for as soon as those polite syllables were uttered, her lips shriveled to the size and texture of a small dried prune. "'Tis a shame your aunt could find no better, more respectable companion for your journey. And that's all I have to say in the matter."

"I appreciate your concern, Mrs. Smith, but I'm sure it will work out very well. Mr. Deverell's private carriage is a vast improvement on the mail coach."

She'd lived in London several months now, long enough to know that few folk there had much good to say of the Deverell family, who were disdainfully considered "new wealth" and upstarts— and those were some of the kindest epithets. But who was Anne Follyot to sneer? She wasn't even "old" wealth.

Deverells, so the saying went, did things differently. They were filthy rich, reputedly shameless, lawless, and mostly unprincipled.

She could not help but think it must be exhausting, not to mention logistically impossible, for a handful of males to "ruin" such a vast number of women and leave quite so much chaos in their wake. They would never have a moment to sleep or read a good book.

As a lover of good stories herself, she was certain a great many tales of Deverell debauchery were entirely made up to keep life interesting for those who told them.

"You're a naive young miss," her landlady muttered. "I wish you had firmer hands to guide you, but it's not my business. I've got enough to do, and it's not my job to act as your mother. You'll end up ruined, no doubt, like many a wide-eyed chit before you. Fancy sending a Deverell for your innocent young niece. Like sending a fox to fetch a hen to market! What can your aunt be thinking?"

"Mrs. Smith, you are a very dear lady to worry so about me. But I am not nearly as helpless as I might look. I am, after all, a woman of the modern age."

Her landlady looked skeptical of this claim. She was not, however, the first person to think Anne a little light in the head— a consequence, perhaps, of her spirits refusing to be crushed under the weight of misfortune. They thought she must live in her own strange, fantasy world, but her feet were quite well grounded in this one. She simply made the best she could of it, which, she had sadly come to realize, made her puzzling and insufferable company to most.

As if to see her happy with so little made their own fortunes decline rapidly.

"You were raised in a one bull country village, Miss Follyot. What do you know of men like Deverells?"

"I know that they pull their breeches on one leg at a time, just as other men do. Men like my father and brother. They have all the same parts and require all the same handling."

The landlady huffed. "I would not be so certain of that. Not from the stories I've heard."

"But I have familiarity with all manner of beasts. I've stared down an escaped seed ox and helped lance an abscess on the ear of a particularly peevish sow more than twice my size. Few things cast any fear in my heart."

"You'll be soft clay in that man's claws, mark my words!"

Before Anne could give any further words of assurance, Mrs. Smith walked into the parlor, still shaking her head, and nudging the door shut swiftly behind her to keep out the cold breeze that blew through the hall of her narrow boarding house. The other young ladies who rented rooms there were gathered around a cheerful fire in that parlor, waiting to enjoy a hot cup of tea and some buttered crumpets. Very likely, in the anticipation of these delights, they had all forgotten about Anne. Not that she was ever very memorable.

Now she was abandoned to whatever gruesome fate awaited her at the hands of a Deverell. The way Mrs. Smith said that name— as if it had to be got out as quickly as possible, under cover of darkness, before curious neighbors witnessed its departure— the syllables rolled together and made it sound like "Devil".

Anne felt a little like the heroine in a Brontë novel, hovering on the cusp of an adventure, unfathomable in its awfulness, bursting with dire and dreadful possibilities. Perhaps something remarkable was finally about to happen to her and this time she would not have to make it up while standing at her wash bowl or peeling potatoes.

She'd had her eye on a length of rose madder silk taffeta from Lockreedy and Velder, you see, but would feel a fraud wearing a gown made of it until she had a reason. Rose madder was not the sort of color associated with plain, ordinary, unexciting girls to whom nothing ever happened.

Her mother had been a no-frills, no-nonsense woman, who did not beat about the bushes to save anybody's feelings.

"Anne, you do better in brown," she would say, whenever she caught her little daughter wistfully perusing jollier shades on the haberdasher's shelves when they went into the nearest town. "It doesn't show stains or make promises you can't deliver. It's steadfast, practical and doesn't try to stand out."

Her mother took every opportunity to pass on such advice, almost as if she'd known her time on earth would not last long enough to see her daughters into adulthood.

Anne quite understood her mother's point about being practical. But, still, that rose madder taffeta called to her with a siren's song and her mother was no longer living to redirect her attention. One of these days, Anne would claim it for her own. Once she'd had an escapade worthy of such color and could truly claim herself to be "modern" and not merely aspiring to the state.

A journey in the company of a Deverell—whispered to let it roll languidly off her tongue and make that candle flame shiver wantonly—was surely the closest to such adventure Anne Follyot would ever come. Something to surpass any other in her one and twenty years. In the eyes of many, like Mrs. Smith, merely being seen in his company was enough to raise her status from commonplace to endangered.

If he came.

Did men like Deverells keep their promises?

She was taking a chance. Being reckless. But life, surely, was not meant to be neatly and tidily laid out, or else there would be no need for things like initiative and imagination.

Anne felt in her coat pocket and took out the letter recently received from her sister, Lizzie. A little whisper of guilt stole through her mind. But no, she had come this far to be free. Now she would take another step for herself, after putting her own needs aside for most of her life. Her sister would simply have to understand. Eventually.

The letter consigned to the depths of her pocket again, she looked out through the frosted window, eager for sign of her infamous escort.

The candle in her cold, stiff fingers would soon be burned down, leaving her in the dark, but she wouldn't want to ask the landlady for another. Mrs. Smith took the matter of candles very seriously. They were distributed once a week, and the boarders were expected to make their ration last, not to play with them extravagantly or foolishly. Anne, however, enjoyed a great deal of reading at night and wrote so many letters to relatives and friends that she had a tendency to burn through her candles much faster than the other girls, leaving herself in the dark for half the week.

"But one always has news to share, Mrs. Smith, and I have many to whom I must tell it all." So what if, occasionally, the letters she wrote portrayed her life as much more exciting than it truly was? Rose madder rather than mouse-hair brown? She wouldn't want to bore anybody.

Anne had several aunts and great-aunts to whom she wrote, and on their behalf it was her duty, she felt, to make the dull and drear seem extraordinary and unique. After all, they could not get about as she could and must rely upon her letters to keep their spirits up.

For Anne there was yet another reason to make her letters far more interesting than her life. She hoped her aunts and great-aunts would eventually see that she was not in need of their romantic schemes, for just as stubbornly as she was bent on adventure, they were intent on quenching the possibility, by finding a husband who might "do for poor Anne". As if it were a competition and such a booby might be found if only one looked hard enough and dug deep enough into the barrel.

The saddest thing about it— yet also the most comical to a girl with a slightly perverse sense of humor— was that none of those dear ladies knew, or even paused to consider, the sort of man she might find desirable. Nevertheless, as soon as her father died, they took up the cause of Anne's lacking romantic prospects as a personal crusade, even going so far as to feign illness or contrive some other dire emergency to lure her across the countryside and have her exhibited like a fattened, beribboned hog at the county fair. Their interest was well-meant, certainly, but cupid's arrow was always so blindly fired that one day it was liable to take out somebody's eye.

Such was the urgency of getting Anne "settled", that even a proper period of mourning was not to be respected. Her father had left strict instructions that he did not expect his children to grieve his passing; he felt that they had all mourned their mother long enough. Perhaps he thought also to spare the expense of more bombazine and crape for the girls, since the gowns they wore when their mother died belonged to childhood and had long since been outgrown in all directions. But the female relatives on her mother's side had seen Tom Follyot's request for shortened mourning as a sign that they should intensify the search for husbands. Only a year after their father's passing, her little sister Lizzie had pleased them by doing what was expected of her. The only thing that had ever been expected of her.

Anne, however, was less easily disposed of.

"Aunt Benjamina," she'd been obliged to ask once across the custard tarts, "is it your intention that I marry the first desperate fellow who can be induced into asking? Papa always assured me that I am free to marry whomever I choose."

"Your father, my dear, was a good man, but his expertise was in beasts of the field and farmyard, not young ladies of one and twenty, who have neither fortune nor great beauty."

Yes, there it was again. In case she forgot.

"No stone unturned then," she replied with a polite smile.

"Quite so. Now, be mindful of this, Anne. You are a serviceable creature, not afraid or unaccustomed to hard work. Keeping house for your father and siblings these past ten years you are well broken in to drudgery, and that is your main attraction— your usefulness. Remember that. A plain, mild tempered bachelor, or a steady, elderly widower, will serve you better than some handsome, charming scoundrel likely to chase after every pretty face that passes. For there will be many prettier and nothing lies in such a man's bed for you except heartache."

She was shocked that Aunt Benjamina would mention a man's bed at all, but apparently the lady was slipping more sherry into her tea than anybody realized. That might also explain the loosened hairpins that stuck out like hedgehog spikes around her head and had entertained Anne's mind for several minutes, while she counted them and imagined her aunt transformed into one of those shy, spiny creatures.

"The right man for you, Anne dear," the hedgehog squeaked, nose twitching above her tea cup, "will be reserved, steadfast, plain and practical."

"And won't show the stains," she muttered.

"What's that, dear?"

"But surely," Anne had persisted, "the right man for me will be one who appreciates a companion with a strong, lively mind. Father always said it was my—"

"No man wants a wife with a mind that is anything but obedient. If your father encouraged you to believe otherwise, he did you a great disservice. But do not be crestfallen. I know how you young girls are and you have not the slightest inkling of what's good for you. Fortunately, my dear, you have *us* to guide you now."

So Anne had taken swift strides to escape all that kindly guidance, by packing her mother's old trunk and boldly arriving in London to live as independently as a young girl could, for as long as she could, and— just to be sure they did not think her abducted by a highwayman for his wicked pleasure— she wrote to her relatives with as much cheerful, busy news as might be created by her pen. She wanted them to know that she lacked for nothing, and managed very well all on her own. That no man was required.

It had not, however, stopped their fretting and matchmaking efforts.

Fortunately, her Aunt Follyot was one of the few rational ladies in the family. She had once dared suggest that Anne could be just as content in her life without a husband as with one, and that she could well afford to wait. An invitation from her, therefore, need not be faced with trepidation. There was no chance that this could be a ruse to get Anne dressed up in her best brown and set before some unfortunate, milksop bachelor, along with the stuffed goose and gravy. For that reason, and since it would be only the second Yuletide without her father— somehow harder than the first— she was very glad to spend this Christmas with her favorite aunt.

If she ever got all the way to Widecombe, of course.

Her candle flame fluttered miserably in the draft, struggling to stay upright. Any moment now it would leave her with naught but a thin trail of smoke and a tiny glowing ember. At least there was a gaslight at the end of the alley, so that even if her flame died out she would still see the silhouette of anybody approaching.

When he came.

If he came.

He might not.

Oh, the waiting was unbearable. Feeling restless, she considered walking outside, down the alley to the street. Anything to pass the time, even though it was cold and icy out there. At least, moving, she would feel as if she did something and was not merely standing passively by waiting for adventure to happen.

She watched the lanterns of the omnibus pass by at the end of the alley, moving swiftly, carrying its huddled passengers to their homes.

Still no sign of the Deverell.

It did not matter, she thought briskly. It really shouldn't matter. She would go into the parlor and have crumpets. Later, in a letter to her aunt, she would laugh at the incident and at her foolishness for waiting so long in the cold dark. The rose madder taffeta must wait a while longer.

A Deverell. Goodness gracious, times must be desperate indeed that they were obliged to rely upon a Deverell.

But Aunt Follyot was a sensible, respectable lady— a vicar's widow—who would not have made such a plan unless the components fitted within it were deemed trustworthy.

"Mrs. Olivia Deverell, has been a loyal friend to me, ever since your dear uncle and I came to Cornwall twenty years ago, to take over the living so kindly offered by my cousin. Now that I am widowed and reside in Widecombe, she still rides over

quite often to visit. When she told me of her son's plans for Christmas and suggested he had room enough to bring you to me on his way, I eagerly accepted on your behalf and on mine. I hope that was not too forward of me?

It will be so lovely to see you, my dear, and I wonder if you are much changed. I know from your letters that your life in London is so very full and exciting now, and I fear that you may think Widecombe society and your widowed aunt's company quite tedious and grim in comparison..."

No more mention of Mr. J.P. Deverell was made other than a line about a Christmas party at her uncle's vicarage, during which Anne may have encountered him when they were children. Being only five at the time, Anne had little memory of it, but she and her brother had been sent to stay with their relatives in Cornwall that year because their mother was sick and in the last weeks of a difficult pregnancy. The doctor in Little Marshes had thought it would improve her strength for the birth to send her other two children out of the way and put them in somebody else's care for a while, thus Anne and her brother were fetched south to the vicarage in Porthwellen, by their uncle and aunt. Once their little sister was born and their mother's health recovered enough, they came home again, their visit to Cornwall soon nothing more than a few wisps of memory for Anne.

Well, she recalled being hit hard by a snowball that Christmas at her Uncle Peter's vicarage and screaming to bring the house down until somebody fed her marzipan and port. If there were any Deverells present they had left no impression greater than the sting of a snowball to the face. In fact, J.P.

Deverell was very probably responsible for that snowball, if everything said of him was true.

She raised a hand to her temple, recalling the wound. Ouch! Yes, his name conjured a quick, flickering image and the echo of that long ago scream.

The flame of her candle went out. She caught her breath.

A shadowy shape suddenly formed at the end of the alley and then proceeded to fill the frosty window as it drew nearer with an uneven gait. At first she thought the beast had three legs, until she realized that one of them was a cane, swung impatiently ahead of him between every step. Sometimes he slipped and then she saw the bristling fog of his breath as he exhaled a curse into the crisp winter's air.

It could be nobody else but the man himself. The Deverell. Gentlemen visitors were not permitted at Mrs. Smith's boarding house, except on errands of urgency, and tradesmen came only in daylight. So who else could it be?

Had the memory of that long ago scream finally summoned the beast from his dark lair?

The relief she felt at seeing him was surprisingly warm, considering she had already told herself that she wouldn't mind if he didn't come. There were, after all, crumpets to be had by way of compensation and now she would have to forgo the treat.

But there he was.

Before he could ring the bell, she swept the door open in anxious haste.

"Mr. J.P. Deverell, I presume?"

He was six foot tall and about as happy as a bull that had somehow got wind of its imminent castration. At least he had the manners to remove his hat and there were no horns visible beneath. But it was a brief gesture, clearly made under duress, and as a tight sigh oozed out of one side of his mouth, he confirmed his identity with a gruff, "Regrettably."

It was instantly clear that there would be no apology for his lack of punctuality, for as his gaze drifted over her smoking candle wick, old brown coat, dented trunk and wicker basket, he exhaled a weary, "You're ready then." A sneer turned up the corner of his mouth. "That's something, at least." As if, because she was a woman, he'd expected much more fuss and fanfare around her departure.

"And you're better late than never," she exclaimed cheerily. "We're doing well already, aren't we?" With that, and holding her basket in the crook of one arm, she reached down for a handle of her trunk. He had begun to turn away, so she said, "Could you be so kind as to get the other? I have not much within it that is of value and tossing it all about will do little harm, but I do hate the noise it makes when it drags along the cobbles."

His lips parted for another plume of breath as he looked back at her. "Why do women require so much baggage?" He looked like a mythical creature, Anne thought suddenly. A dragon whose flames were temporarily dampened and reduced to puffs of smoke. Before she could respond, he bent and grabbed the other handle— so violently that it came away with a spirited crack.

"Ah. I fear my trunk was quite unprepared for such a forceful handling," she murmured, looking at the broken, bent and now useless brass ring in Deverell's large fist. "It is generally accustomed to a more delicate grip. I just had that handle re-affixed too, alas!"

"Apparently the job was not done well enough."

"Take pity on my poor trunk, sir, for it is much older than I and has, I believe, traveled mostly in the service of maiden aunts, postulant nuns and missionaries' wives. I suppose you'll be quite a shock to it."

He glowered down at her. "And vice versa." The words rumbled out of him on another cloud of mist and then he tossed the broken handle across the alley, thrust his cane at her to catch and lifted the trunk onto his shoulder, as if it weighed as much as a sack of feathers. "Why do you stand there gawping, woman? One foot before the other, if you please. If you can manage that much on your dainty stumps. I haven't all damnable night and if you imagine I might be prevailed upon to carry you too, let me disabuse you of the notion."

Having balanced her trunk thus, he limped away toward the lamp post, his coat flapping around him like the wings of a raven, speckled with glittering snowflakes that had already begun to form a crust upon his shoulder until her trunk displaced them.

She was very tempted to go back inside and eat crumpets. Dreadful, rude man!

But suddenly she felt a warmer whisper of air against the back of her neck and knew that somebody had opened the parlor door, just a crack, to peek around it. They were all most curious, naturally, about the Deverell at the door. They must wonder how she, plain Miss Anne Follyot, previously of Little Marshes, Oxfordshire— population forty-nine, and all her business, or lack of it, known to them, as theirs was to her—and owner of mostly brown garments, had any connection to such a man.

For once she was a person of interest.

Anne recovered her breath, lifted her chin and decided that despite his surly lack of manners there was nothing else to be done, but follow the Deverell.

For the sake of her abused and kidnapped trunk, if for no other reason.

Besides, she wanted adventure, did she not? There was not a moment to waste if she was to get away before Lizzie arrived and ended all hope of excitement.

Perhaps she would accomplish just a smidgen of rose madder scandal, before she was too old to have any and they buried her in brown.

Chapter Four

"I am Miss Anne Follyot," she said, offering her hand to shake. She thought that he— a man of solemn business and gravest frown— would appreciate a straightforward, bold, modern manner. "But I suppose you know that already. Oh, dear!" She laughed nervously. "I've never been in this situation before, so I am not entirely sure how to proceed. We have been introduced already, according to my aunt, but it was many years ago, I fear." Since he had done nothing with her gloved hand except stare at it with mild disdain and then severe distrust, she stretched it forward another few, brave inches. "You hit me in the face with a snowball when I was five."

He paused, squinting at her over his scarf.

"But I hereby bury the hatchet." She smiled. "Perhaps you were not aiming at me at all. I have been told that I do not particularly stand out. But I do talk too much. You must tell me if I begin to give you a sore head, and I shall try to hold my tongue. How do you do, sir?"

He growled, "I've done better." Finally grasping her fingertips with the same force as he'd broken her trunk handle, he shook her hand once and left it numb. "The trunk will have to go on the outside. I'll tie it." He waved both his arms at her as if she were an escaped hog to be corralled. "Get in then. Go on with you. Stop standing there like a simpleton."

She'd never seen a gentleman tying a trunk to a carriage. They usually left such labor to others. But J.P. Deverell, Esq.— as his single leather attaché case proclaimed in worn gilt letters— did not appear to live by the customary rules. Or manners. Despite his limp he was surprisingly capable, working alongside his coachman to secure her trunk with a length of rope.

"Haste," he barked, when he found her still standing in the falling snow, gazing up at him. "Unless you mean to freeze your damnable stockings off. Can't have you getting frostbite on top of everything else, for I suppose I'd be blamed for that too."

So she complied, taking a seat inside with her wicker basket and his cane. A moment later he joined her and they were off, his horses tearing into the crisp evening like rough hands cleaving a length of star-studded silk.

The man was evidently determined to be as unpleasant and discouraging as possible. He could not be that brusque and ill-mannered all the time, surely? Anne remembered how her brother used to get into dreadful sulks as a child. Usually treacle pudding and custard would get him out of it again eventually, which was probably why he'd grown into a distinctly portly gentleman, out of breath whenever he was required to move far from his chair or mount many more steps than two. But she had no treacle pudding at hand with which to feed the petulant child seated opposite. In any case, Anne, unlike her mother, did not believe in rewarding bad behavior.

"You have no luggage of your own, sir?" she inquired politely of her escort, nodding at the leather case. "Other than that, which looks like work of a sort. At Christmas."

Although it was surely too dark to read, she had seen the quick flare of silver when he produced a pen knife from inside his coat and now he used it to cut open the pages of a newspaper. "Why not at Christmas? What's so different about that?" he growled.

"Well, it's...it's—" she shrugged, "—Christmas."

As they rumbled along beside park railings, a trembling drift of moonlight and shadows—bare tree limbs, tangled and knotted— reached into the carriage and sketched him with the thick black slashes of a broken charcoal pencil. "And thus the world stops turning?" He put his pen knife away and shook out his paper, lifting it between them. "Commerce grinds to a halt?"

"Of course it does not stop altogether. But I'm sure even Mr. Lockreedy comes out of his office at Christmas."

There was a lengthy pause, during which she wondered if he had fallen asleep behind his paper. Then, finally, his face still concealed behind that barrier, he murmured, "And who the devil might Mr. Lockreedy be?"

"My employer, sir. He runs a very successful shop. Lockreedy and Velder's Universal Emporium on Grand Street. You must have heard of it."

"I cannot say that I have."

"He works long hours up in his office above the shop, but even he celebrates Christmas. I know because I saw brandy and mince pies taken up there today by the head clerk."

"Did you indeed?" he murmured as if he barely listened and had found something much more interesting to read.

"Mr. Shepherd, the head clerk, is the only person allowed up there. He communicates between us — the underlings who work for him— and the mysterious Mr. Lockreedy, who so few have ever seen."

"Is that so?"

"I have concluded that he suffers a peculiar disease which demands that he stay in the dark and never venture into daylight. Or else he is scarred by war. The other girls dared me once to hide under his desk before he came in, so that I could see what he looked like and whether he really wears a black hooded cloak to hide his disfigurement, as we suspect he does. So I came to work very early a few weeks ago, but the door was locked and then I heard snoring inside. Would you believe it?" She sighed and shook her head. "The poor fellow must sleep in his office."

He shuffled his paper. "Perhaps he hangs upside down in there like a bat."

"It shows great dedication to his work, but one cannot help but worry for his health."

"Why would you worry about him? I doubt he knows you exist."

Since this was probably quite true she could not argue with it. There was another pause, and then she said, "It is very good of you to bring me along on your trip."

"I didn't."

"I beg your pardon?"

"I didn't bring you along on *my* trip. I had no reason of my own to go out. This is *your* trip, Miss Follyot. Solely for you."

"Oh. I hope you did not have other plans."

"What does that matter? Whatever they were, I must now set them aside. Not for the first time."

"I am grieved," she exclaimed.

"And I am accustomed to incommodious events."

"I would not have put you out like this, had I known."

"Never mind." He sighed heftily into his newspaper.

"But my aunt thought you were traveling in any case, to see your family. Now I am a great encumbrance."

"We must grin and bear the hardship as best we can. It's Christmas, so I'm told. A season rife with nuisances."

Anne shook her head. "You may put this nuisance down at the next inn. I'm sure I can find passage on the mail coach."

"Of course." He snorted behind his paper. "I'd never hear the last of it if I dropped you on your behind now and cast you to the mercies of the public coach, would I? Typical of a Deverell. But if that's what you prefer, by all means. I do not suppose Jarvis and the horses will object to being put to and back again in this weather for so little purpose, and any inconvenience to myself is nothing."

She swiftly decided to say no more about getting out. In truth, she had no desire to ride in the mail coach, even if it might be possible to procure a seat this late in the day. Despite the incivility of her companion, the journey in his carriage would be less tiresome and uncomfortable than it could have been, crowded in with less savory folk. At least this man was clean and not malodorous, and apparently intent on keeping the wall of newspaper between them. She could move her elbows freely, which might seem a small bonus, but was actually a gift of tremendous proportion, acknowledged by anybody who ever had cause to travel by stage or mail coach.

Settling back in her seat, she glanced down at his knee. It did not seem to be a permanent injury, for the bandage was tied in haste and slapdash, spotted with a little dried blood, which suggested his trousers beneath were torn. So he had not changed his clothes, or taken any concern over his grooming before coming out to fetch her. If Anne was not already assured of his complete disinterest, that tattered bandage would have told her that he had no care for her opinion. Or possibly for anybody's.

She, on the other hand, had been so anxious to make a good impression on her infamous traveling companion that she'd even had her trunk cleaned, fixed, and relined— despite the fact that he would never see the inside of it. For an entire week she'd been mentally packing and unpacking, fretting over a hole in her hatband and thinking how best to disguise it.

Such a journey, for her, was quite a remarkable thing. For him it meant nothing more than an irritation.

Anne stared out at the swirling snow, clutching her basket as they went over a hard bump. She felt deflated, which was most unlike her, for she could generally find something humorous in any event. This, however, was a tragedy of magnificent proportion. If there was one thing she hated being, it was an inconvenience, an object in everybody's way.

"My aunt will be as sorry as I am for putting you to this service and upsetting your Christmas plans. I wonder how she could have misunderstood. It is not like her at all."

Her ungallant escort remained huddled behind his newspaper, the cold air rising off him in stiff hackles. "I can assure you my mother has some part in it. She's been trying to find a reason to get me home."

She returned her gaze to his newspaper, surprised. "You need a reason to see your family other than Christmas?"

"I have a very busy working life. It does not come to a halt for sickness, death or Christmas." He sighed. "As for family, I would rather visit Roscarrock Castle when there are not likely to be other folk milling about." It was as if the words were torn out of him while he gritted his teeth, trying to hold them in and ripping them to shreds in the process. "Being ceaselessly *merry* about the place."

Anne would have chuckled, but he gave no encouragement. Perhaps he did not mean to amuse her. Perhaps he had no idea how amusing he was. In the darkness she could not tell. The carriage's outside lamps were positioned to light the road ahead and gave nothing to the passengers but a very thin, ghostly shower of amber every so often as they turned a corner.

"Roscarrock Castle sits on its own island off the Cornish coast, does it not?" she ventured. "I saw it once in a picture and thought how beautiful it was. Wild and rugged and a little bit frightening; a thing that seemed not to be built by man, but grown naturally out of the rock on which it stood. I heard once that it is haunted by a previous resident who carries his head under one arm. I suppose he needs it to tell him where he's going. If it were me I would probably set the head down somewhere and forget where I put it."

"I'm sure it would still keep talking until you found it again."

"Ah, but I spot a dilemma, sir. How would I hear it? The ears are on the head." When he made no reply, she continued, "How wonderful it must be to grow up in such an extraordinary place as Roscarrock Castle. Like having your own medieval sovereignty that, when the tide is in, can only be reached by boat." She imagined herself waving from a high turret, her hair much longer than necessary, blowing like a pennant in the sea breeze, as a knight galloped across the sands to her rescue before the tide came in.

"My father certainly considers it his kingdom."

"Which makes you a prince," she exclaimed. "Fancy that! Anne Follyot escorted into Cornwall by a prince." She leaned forward to whisper at his newspaper. "I must mind my slippers."

"Why is that, Miss Follyot?" he murmured wearily behind the pages.

"Girls tend to leave their slippers behind when they meet princes, don't they?"

"Then I would advise that you keep yours tied to your ankles and your feet on the ground, for there is no prince in this carriage."

Anne watched his gloved fingers clasped tightly around the paper and remembered how hard, and yet oddly comforting, his grip had felt around her hand. She sat back again and looked down at her own fingers. They still trembled a little from that brief contact. As if she'd known it before.

"In any case, thank you, sir," she said, somberly. "Prince or toad, however it came about that you agreed to take me, I am very grateful. I must find a way to repay your kindness."

He grunted, shoulders shifting, paper rustling. "Unnecessary."

"Of course it's necessary!"

"I pray you, madam, never burden your tiny brain cells with it again."

"But such a tremendous favor must be reimbursed."

"If it's a favor, what's the bloody point of paying it back? It's not a favor then, is it? If you insist on paying it back, then I'll have to do the same in return and so on and so forth. There'll be no end to it and we'll go to our graves still trying to repay each other. So sit still and be thankful in silence. Strike it from your mind. Dismiss it from your damnable thoughts. We'll both be better off for it."

Again she almost laughed, but fearing he was deadly serious– or so it seemed— she curbed the impulse.

"I suppose your delicate ears are offended," he added. "My language, I am told, is not fit for the best drawing rooms."

"My ears may as well get accustomed to it, since we're trapped together for the next few days," she replied, sanguine. "Besides, I'm not fit for the best drawing rooms myself. I'm told I have an air of the unforgivably cheerful maladroit about me. What do you suppose that means, exactly?"

"One hesitates to imagine."

Wiping her breath from the carriage window, she peered out. "I was not enormously thrilled at the prospect of travel in winter either, I must confess, but now that we're on our way I feel quite jolly. Christmas in my aunt's company will certainly be preferable to eating over-boiled, under-salted potatoes and thin, tasteless gravy in Mrs. Smith's kitchen. She's not the best of cooks, my landlady. Even mice don't care for the crumbs of her pastry, the poor little things."

Anne did not think he was listening at all now, but as she paused for breath, he remarked, "Those *poor little things* spread disease, Miss Follyot."

"Many things spread disease. Including people. Mice are unfairly put upon. We are all God's creatures."

He gave a low groan behind his newspaper. "That's who's to blame, is it?"

"My father was a country veterinarian, Mr. Deverell. Large animal practice. He taught me to respect and value all forms of life. Unfortunately, this has led to more than a few screams, fits of the vapors and petticoat-clinging dances from Mrs. Smith who does not share my love for *wretched creatures*, as she calls them."

"Your landlady has my deepest sympathies."

"As I told her, even she should stop waging war against her enemies at Christmas and spread good will to all living creatures. This is a time for peace and tolerance."

"Peace? Yes, wouldn't that be nice?"

She watched the crackling wall of newspaper between them. It was no good. She simply had to say..."You cannot possibly see to read, Mr. Deverell. You will ruin your eyesight."

He finally looked up over the edge of his page. Briefly lighting the shadows of winter's early night, his eyes glittered with a curious intensity. The silvery moon's passing caress traced the rumpled pleats of his brow, treating her to further hints and clues about her reluctant traveling companion. "And why is this of concern to you?"

"Because I'm sure you have lovely eyes. When they stop scowling at print in the dark."

For a moment all was quiet. Awkwardly so. Perhaps she should not have said "lovely". It was not the sort of word one used for a grown man's eyes, was it? Besides, she had hardly seen his. They were strangers. She was over-excited, too forward. The unforgivably cheerful maladroit.

"What's wrong with you then?" he muttered abruptly, shutting his paper and folding it, apparently giving up on pretending to read.

"What's wrong with me? What can you mean, sir?" Had he been talking to her brother, who wanted her packed off to an asylum?

He tossed the paper to the seat beside him. "My mother's letter described you as sickly." As they passed the glow of another gas lamp, his gaze swept down and up. "But you don't look ill at all," he snapped. "Indeed, I would describe you as bursting with... vitality."

It was, possibly, the closest thing to a compliment she would ever get from such a man, Anne realized. But, of course, he did not mean for it to be anything of the sort. "I am not sick," she assured him steadily. "I am in excellent health, as far as I know."

He ground his jaw, shook his head and turned his angry, critical glare to the snowy shapes beyond the carriage window.

She watched his profile thoughtfully as it fluttered in and out of light. He reminded her a little of that castle in which he was born on the tiny island of Roscarrock. His was an arrogant, rough-hewn, haunted, reluctant beauty— the sort that silly girls often swooned over, much to the utter disdain and puzzlement of those who possessed it. Anne herself was not a swooner, few things struck fear in her heart, and even fewer men left her breathless in admiration. She'd always imagined that if she ever fell in love at all, it would be with the ugliest of toads. Her brother, Wilfred, and various aunts would say that Anne was just contrary enough to prefer an amphibian.

"Are you disappointed to find me so far from death's door, sir?"

He muttered under his breath, "I do not like to be made a fool. I was– no doubt mischievously— informed you were sickly and that it was urgent you get safely to your aunt."

"Gracious. And thus you were induced to ride to my rescue?"

A low huff oozed out of him, as if his working parts wound down slowly and painfully.

Searching for another subject, Anne pointed to his knee. "What happened there, sir? You are injured, I see."

"Some damn fool left a trunk in the street today to trip me up."

"They did it deliberately?"

He growled, "Very likely."

"Oh, dear. It must hurt," she said, lowering her voice sympathetically.

"On the contrary," he snapped. "It feels delightful. I'm thinking of having the same forceful blow applied to the other knee."

"At least then they'd match."

That surprised him. She saw his eyes flare, moonlight bursting into silvery flame in their depths. "You need not feign concern for my knee, Miss Follyot. I will deliver you safely to your aunt and that is all. There is no need for you to form any... unwise attachment."

"Unwise attachment?" she exclaimed.

"This is the season when folk often act in a manner that is not themselves and they acquire romantic ideas. Christmas does not have that effect upon me, however. You may as well be warned."

She wrinkled her nose. How funny he was! "Can a young lady not inquire politely about a wounded leg, without that leading to an *attachment*?"

"I shall save you the trouble of nurturing any such idea about this journey. It has surely occurred to you that my mother and your aunt have conspired to thrust us together in this fashion for their own peculiar amusement."

"Amusement?"

"You are a young woman in reduced circumstances and in need of a husband —"

"According to whom?" she exclaimed.

"I merely state the obvious facts, madam. Is it not the purpose of all women beyond a certain age, that they marry?"

"I do not believe my sensible Aunt Follyot would resort to—"

"A Deverell for her innocent niece?"

"I was going to say romantic machinations, sir."

He huffed, arms folded over his chest. "Well, if you wish to be naive, far be it from me to open your eyes to their games. Play along into their trap, by all means, but do not expect me to join you. I've had enough women slapping me around the face and breaking china over my head, when my plans do not suit their own, and then declaring me, loudly to the rest of the world, a rake and a seducer."

Astonished by this venomous outpouring, she replied, "I asked about your leg to be polite. It would have been odd if I avoided the subject, I suppose. But I can assure you, I do not care if it falls off altogether."

He didn't look as if he believed her. In the flutter of a passing lantern, she saw his lips twitch and his eyes narrow, their own flame dimmed. At least his rage had subsided. But was he amused, or angry? Or simply smug? Usually adept at reading faces, his was two-thirds mystery to her, being cloaked in the darkness between lanterns and moon beams.

"With your reputation, Mr. Deverell," she said carefully, "you're supposed to be the one who tries to seduce me. And here I find you afraid that it might be the other way about."

"I didn't say I was afraid. I said you'd be wasting your time."

She should never have used the word "lovely" about his eyes, or talked teasingly of princes. It had given him quite the wrong idea about her, and apparently he was the only soul allowed to be sarcastic. Anne pressed her knees more tightly together and turned slightly on her seat.

"Then perhaps it will put you at ease to know that I have a fiancé, sir."

"My mother's letter made no mention of it."

"Because my aunt is unaware at present. I mean to surprise her with the news. So, there you have it. I cannot speak for the intentions of the rest of the world, especially if you always go about in it carrying that sizeable air of grievance across your shoulders, your menacing frown inspiring flights of fancy in the minds of a certain sort of woman, but you are quite safe from any wicked plan of seduction on my account."

"Why could this finance not transport you across the country then?"

"He is in the north."

"The north? Pole?"

"He has business. In... Derbyshire."

"I see. May I know the name of this fortunate fellow, so that I might congratulate him should we meet?"

"Mr. Dar—" she glanced out of the window "— winters. Mr. Claiborne Arbuthnot Darkwinters. The third. Of Basingstoke."

"Sounds entirely feasible."

"He's a very fine gentleman."

"As befits his name."

"He would have brought me to my aunt if he did not have important business to tend."

"How could I be in any doubt?"

As the space lengthened between glimpses of the moon and lighted windows again, he sat back, his face disappearing into the swathes of darkness, but now that he'd unfolded his arms again she could make out the shape of his gloved hands, the fingers long and clawed on his thighs, perched there restlessly like the talons of an eagle or some other, savage bird of prey.

"Mr. Darkwinters is very well respected in his field," she said.

"Fallow or wheat?"

"Exploration. He's an explorer. He discovers things."

"As he discovered you, apparently."

"He digs up bones, pots, ancient treasure and such."

"In Basingstoke?"

"A man might have just as many adventures in Basingstoke as anywhere. But he travels a great deal to many other exciting places too. India, Egypt, Mongolia, the Argentine. Wales."

"No wonder he is too busy to bring you to Widecombe, Miss Follyot. I am only surprised he found the time to be engaged at all."

After a pause, she said, "You are a solicitor, are you not, sir?"

"Not."

"Oh, I thought you were."

"I have a half-brother in that profession, although he resides in America. Why? Do you seek legal advice?"

"I simply try to make conversation."

"Is it necessary?"

"It will be a long journey to suffer without it."

Anne heard another blistering sigh.

"What business are you in then, sir?" she pressed.

"Nothing that would interest you."

"How can you know that?"

No reply.

Not discouraged, she continued, "One of your brothers manages a gentleman's club called Deverell's, and another brother is a famed Naval hero, who, they say, bought his wife at a bride sale, is that true?"

"There are altogether too many half-siblings and all a great deal older than me. I'm afraid I don't keep reins on any."

"And your only sister is the Countess of Southerton?"

"Much to the distress of the upper classes, who never quite got accustomed to the outrage."

"Because your father was a foundling who made his fortune from gambling?" And was divorced from his first wife. And raised all his children together, whether legitimate or bastard born, on that little kingdom out at sea. But she thought better of adding all that. He probably did not need reminding of his family's eccentricities.

"Why so many questions, shop girl?"

"Just curious, sir. You and I may never meet again, in which case this could be the only opportunity I shall ever have to ask a Deverell, in person. It would be remiss of me not to seize upon it while we have all this time together." Feeling a sudden spark of wickedness, she could not resist adding, "While I have you trapped, so to speak." She bit her lip. "They tell me that Deverells do things differently."

His fingers tapped upon his thigh, then stilled again like a crouched spider. "Let me make it plain for you, Miss Follyot, and save your questions. My family is a novel in which the characters wrestle the pen from the author's fingers and spill ink. Or a traveling circus in which the beasts overrun the cages to maul the audience. You would be better off not buying a ticket. Bolt your doors and windows when they come to town."

She thought about this for a moment and then said, "You must be the sore-tempered, dancing bear then."

"Yes," he growled. "But without the dancing, only the temper. So be warned."

"Fortunately, I have experience with wounded strays, and a childhood spent trudging along after my father on farm visits taught me how to handle beasts of all sizes and temperaments. I am particularly familiar with the tools of castration." She smiled pleasantly. "So perhaps you're right to be wary of me. Although not for the reasons you so readily assume."

Another flare of moonlight touched his face, and she was rewarded by the quickening of something new that wiped the smug haughtiness from his countenance. Surprise and panic. Or amusement.

She'd take either. It was a beginning and an advance on cold disinterest.

Chapter Five

He had expected a thin, small, pale, ghostly woman in a veil. Why he'd added the veil in his imagination he couldn't say— it was not like him to be frivolous with lace— but for some reason it had seemed appropriate.

Miss Follyot, however, did not fit the picture he'd conjured with the aid of his mother's few lines of description. For one thing she was far too chatty, being in possession of too much healthy breath. Neither his long silences, nor his brusque replies, discouraged her rambling wit.

The brief sighting of her face in moonlight had suggested a round shape, freckled and full of expression, not sophisticated enough to hide her thoughts. Not the sort of face he generally looked at twice.

Even if she had not mentioned a childhood in the country, he would have guessed it, for there was a proud, unashamed aura of the provincial about Miss Follyot. Her coat— what he could see of it— was constructed in plain cut and fabric, and her hat a simple affair, the dull color lifted by the addition of a single holly sprig tucked into the brown ribbon. There was something familiar about that ugly bonnet.

A veil, he suspected, would only have got in her way and been torn aside impatiently, so that she could watch the snow and not have her view spoiled. She constantly wiped foggy breath from the window to see out, as if something miraculous might happen and she was afraid to miss it. Like a puppy watching its first snowfall and waiting eagerly to be let out in it.

At one point, Miss Follyot seemed to be laughing at him— trying to hide it, but on the verge of hysterics at something he said. It had crossed his mind that he might have soot, ink, or some other mark upon his face that induced her strange merriment, but a sly sweep with his fingers behind the mask of that newspaper had given no clue. And in such dim light, how could she see? He would have to wait until they stopped at a tavern to change horses and then, in some polished surface, assess his reflection for potential comedic value.

"There was a vicarage tea party for the village children some sixteen or seventeen years ago. Perhaps you will remember little Anne?"

How could he? Why would he? At thirteen or fourteen he was only just becoming interested in females as anything other than a target for mud balls and his catapult, and it seemed highly unlikely that he would have found the vicar's plain niece at all memorable.

A vicarage tea party, put on for the children of tiny Porthwellen village, would have been a nightmare for J.P. He did not care for children, even when he was one. No doubt his mother had forced him to dress up in a stiff collar and a hat. It would have been one of her lessons on "behaving like a gentleman". She was very keen on those. But, as a Deverell, one had a reputation before it was even earned.

His mother had also worried that, with siblings all so much older, he spent too much time alone with his books; as a result, painful social outings like vicarage tea parties with other children his age, or younger, were forced upon him with terrifying regularity whenever he was home from school.

He tried to remember this event from boyhood, but saw only flickering candlelight on a Christmas tree— the first he'd ever seen— and oranges. Yes, oranges with cloves stuck in them and wrapped in scarlet ribbon. He recalled the sweet fragrance.

He looked across the carriage again at his noisy passenger. Hit her in the face with a snowball, did he? He supposed it was possible. If his mother knew, he would have received a stern lecture and been made to apologize at once. *A proper gentleman does not hit ladies in the face with snowballs*, she would have said. Or something like it. His father would simply have clipped him 'round the ear

Later, of course, he found that there were women who preferred his *un*gentlemanly side, and they were unchallenging women to be around. They needed little from him— certainly not polite conversation or manners. They preferred him on his worst behavior. Thus, many of his mother's lessons were stored away like dusty books in the attic, forgotten.

Apparently, the vicarage tea party was one of those memories packed away among the cobwebs.

Across his carriage Miss Follyot continued humming happily to herself. It was a song he vaguely recognized as a seasonal carol, marginally more bearable than Good King Wenceslas, despite the general tunelessness. Occasionally she paused to exclaim something about the ice and snow, which she saw as "magical", rather than a cold, slippery inconvenience. His silences did not appear to trouble her at all. Why should they, when she could chatter away easily on a myriad of unconnected subjects and without prompting, that little sprig of holly nodding away in her hat ribbon the entire time?

Again, that bonnet...where had he seen it before? When the holly moved, he could see it partially hid a moth-hole in the ribbon. Even more familiar.

Damn you, Jacob Dockery, this is your fault. His friend must be laughing now, of course, for he knew how little patience J.P. spared for women who talked too much.

"What you need, old chap," Jacob had once pronounced, "is a bouncing, lively creature to smack a smile onto that dour face of yours. Instead, you attach yourself to pretty sloths who spend their time in a reclining state, cannot add two numbers together, except when it comes to the money you give them, and whose greatest fear is a wrinkle."

"Why would I want anything more than that?" he'd replied. Complications ensued when two people climbed out of bed to share conversation.

And "bouncing" creatures, like India rubber balls, were a danger to one's footing and liable to leave bruises.

But if he did not perform this service, with the minimum of offensive remarks uttered, and deliver Miss Follyot safely to her aunt in Widecombe, he would never hear the end of it. His mother had accused him, more than once, of being ungallant and rude to her friends. Just because he refused to flatter falsely or lie arbitrarily.

"You can make an effort for three days, old chap," Dockery whispered in his ear. *"You won't have to see her again, after this. You've managed to ignore her long enough. I'm sure you can go on doing so."*

What the devil did that mean?

Jacob Dockery liked riddles as much as he liked gambling on terrible odds. He had always been the effusive, ebullient face of their partnership, the one everybody adored and found delightfully charismatic. He and J.P. met as schoolboys and very soon the dark, quiet, serious young man and the fair, noisy one were seldom apart, despite their chalk and cheese personalities. They remained close through their university years, when they brewed and sold ale together. Later they came up with the idea to start a business of their own. When Jacob's father died, leaving him a small shop that was desperately in debt. J.P. funded the money to put the business back on its feet and slowly they expanded, changing the name, redecorating, exporting goods from all over the country and abroad. J.P. had kept to the background, working out of sight and usually in silence, grateful to his friend for the shield. Jacob had wanted to call their partnership Deverell and Dockery— or vice versa— but J.P. did not want his name involved, knowing that it came with ready-packaged, unfavorable notoriety. So between them they had come up with the anagram, Lockreedy & Velder.

While his friend represented the charming face of the business, all was well, but now that Dockery was gone, J.P.— the unsociable brain of the partnership— must rely upon buffers, such as Shepherd, his head clerk, between himself and the world.

Consequently, he paid no attention to the girls hired by his head clerk. He trusted Shepherd to read their references and assess their potential. Perhaps he ought to pay more heed in future. But that would mean involving himself in details, in other people's lives.

So she'd been sneaking about trying to get under his desk, had she? He was darkly amused to think of the disappointing shock she would have received to find only him there. Not a cloaked monster. Just a man.

Her fingertips tapped against the wicker lid of her basket as she hummed under her breath.

He suspected that in order to silence her he'd have to find the switch, lever or little button somewhere under her clothes, and she, relative of postulants and missionaries— also familiar, as she boasted, with the tools of castration— was not likely to allow that liberty on a carriage ride to Cornwall.

Better make the effort of conversation. Painful and unpracticed as it was.

Stretching out first his wounded knee and then the other, he said, "What brings a country veterinarian's daughter to London, all on her own, Miss Follyot?"

"I'm a modern girl, sir," she replied proudly. "When my father died last year and my brother put up the house for sale, I knew I had better make my own way in the world. So I wrote to relatives and my first post was as companion to a lady by the name of Mrs.—well, I shall call her Mrs. M. But she did not like me. Thought I talked too much."

"Impossible, surely."

"In truth, sir, I was quite relieved when she gave me my notice, for it is not easy juggling the visits of so many gentlemen and ensuring that none get to know of the others' existence. Most of the time I felt like a chamber maid stuck in a restoration farce about a merry divorcee."

He stared. "Really?" A sudden vision of himself tossing a hat at some fumbling young woman and then, before she stood upright again, growling at her to get out and shut the door, came into his mind. He had barely looked at her, but she was dressed for the outdoors and he now recalled the moth hole in her brown bonnet ribbon.

"I asked her once, how she managed to keep all her gentlemen callers in order and she told me that she named each of them after the seven deadly sins. I would have thought the days of the week more appropriate. But she was amused by her own system. An old maiden aunt of hers had once given her a sampler, embroidered with a warning about the seven sins. I daresay this was her way of biting a thumb at that well-meaning relative."

Alas, he remembered the sampler. Mrs. Marvington kept it framed on her bedchamber wall and frequently laughed at it. At the time he had not realized *why* she was laughing, or that he was part of the joke.

"I see." He felt his frown deepening, his ears getting hot. Which of the seven did that lady name him, he wondered.

"In any case, she sent me off and I applied for a place at Lockreedy and Velder's Universal Emporium. I had passed the window many times, especially to admire a particularly gorgeous rose madder silk on display, but never dared go in. Then I decided, nothing ventured, nothing gained. I certainly did not want my independence lost before it had properly been found."

He nodded slowly.

"The hours of work are much more agreeable than they would be if I went into service, and Mr. Lockreedy is a generous employer, even if he is a recluse. I did not much fancy factory work. That did not appeal to me as much as a shop, where nothing is the same day after day and I can meet new people."

"And talk their ears blue," he mused aloud.

"And wrap things in paper. I do so love to wrap things in paper. It is almost as pleasant as unwrapping them, don't you think? The crinkle and crackle of the paper? The concealing of a mystery and then the unveiling of it." She gazed out at the moon with wonder and excitement, as if it was the first time she'd ever laid eyes upon it. "I do love a good mystery."

Sometimes she seemed to be talking to herself, as much as to him. There was a dreamy quality to her voice and it drew him in, despite his reluctance.

"So the boarding house in which you now reside is only for ladies?"

"Yes. Mrs. Smith is a widow and she runs the house exclusively for the female employees at Lockreedy and Velder."

"A comfortable place?"

"The rooms are clean and Mrs. Smith does not drink gin all day, so I suppose that makes it one of the better boarding houses in London. Indeed, she is a very respectable woman, despite what some of the girls say."

He squinted across the carriage, trying to see her expression. "What do they say?"

"They like to pretend that Mrs. Smith is Mr. Lockreedy's clandestine mistress. I told them it is quite ridiculous and they should not besmirch the poor lady's reputation in that manner."

"But what makes them believe such a thing?"

"Mrs. Smith claims never to have met the man. She protests it so virulently that she only rouses their suspicions further. It has become something of a sport in the house, to try and catch her out, make her confess." She leaned forward as if to share a confidence, despite the fact that they were alone. "Young women can be terribly dangerous and wicked when bored, Mr. Deverell, and the winter months are most treacherous because they are stuck indoors for long hours, the night coming so early."

"I have often suspected as much."

She sat back again. "But even if it were true, I would not blame Mrs. Smith. At her time of life and being widowed, I daresay she needs company of that sort from time to time. Who has a right to forbid companionship between two consenting old people? It does no harm to anybody and makes their advanced years so much happier. What else is she supposed to do, sit in a corner and wait for death? One should make the most of one's life and enjoy every moment."

He cleared his throat of the chuckle that lurked there. "He's an old man then, your Mr. Lockreedy?"

"What else could he be? Close your eyes and say the name. I guarantee you will see a little old grey man in a kilt and a tam o'shanter."

"*A kilt?*" he exclaimed.

"He's a Scotsman, of course, with hairy knees. It stands to reason. And although Mrs. Smith will claim no more than five and thirty years, I would say she is nearer fifty, if she's a day. It could be her last chance for romance. If it is all true."

J.P. scratched his ear and frowned. "But I thought you said, Mr. Lockreedy is a recluse who never comes out of his office."

She did not falter. "I expect he comes out sometimes, when nobody's looking. He would have to, wouldn't he?"

He eyed her shadow cautiously across the carriage. "You have had no dealings with him yourself?"

"Oh, from time to time I send him notes, advising him on little things I think he might consider."

He rubbed his chin. "Advising him? Notes?"

"Yes, on matters of shop display and such. Also items that might improve conditions for his employees." She sighed gustily. "He never answers my notes, of course, and it may be that they are simply trampled underfoot. But occasionally I see my ideas put into action and I daresay that ought to be satisfaction enough for me." She paused. "Although I am left to wonder whether he actually reads my ideas. It would be nice to know he appreciates them, but perhaps that is too much to hope for." She wiped the window clear of her breathy sighs again. "I do hope he is not offended by my ideas. They are sent with every good will in the world and not meant as criticism. After all, I speak to customers every day and he does not."

So this was "A.F.", the mysterious note-sender, whose short, folded missives he occasionally found slid under the office door. He'd assumed they were some sort of prank by Shepherd and had amused himself trying to work out what the initials stood for. "Well... I'm glad your employer and your landlady conduct their affair with discretion, being in charge of so many young, innocent and impressionable ladies."

"But it is probably not true at all and merely the result of too many young ladies cooped up and restless. As I said, Mrs. Smith is most respectable and fusses over us like a mother hen around her chicks." He heard the smile in her voice. "One is obliged to overlook the rather uninspired food offerings, when balanced against the fact that the meals are hot, the building has a stout roof, laundry service is provided for nine-pence a week and we have damaged cake for tea on Sunday. Left over from the shop, of course. Yes, I am happy there. My situation could be much worse."

"Could it?" She was irrepressibly optimistic, he mused. No good could possibly come of such a rosy outlook on life. But she'd learn. She was young yet and the knocks would come to take the shine off. "You have brothers and sisters?"

"One of each. A brother who is older and a sister who is younger. Both married. The sister only just." She exhaled a hearty sigh, shoulders sagging. "At *sixteen*. I would have advised her against it so young, but I knew that would only make her more decided. We have a stubborn streak in our family. Besides, now that our father is gone, she and I had to find places out of the house before our brother sold it. And she is far too ornamental to be useful. It was inevitable she would marry. Mr. George Ingram seems an amiable enough fellow. I suppose he cannot help the shape of his head."

"You could not—what ails the man's head?"

"It is bulbous with a prominent forehead, which suggests weakness and a spendthrift nature, so Mrs. Culpepper says."

"Mrs. Culpepper?"

"The blacksmith's mother in Little Marshes. She will tell you your fortune in the tea leaves for tuppence. For a shilling she'll make it a good one."

"I see...well, if I am ever in the vicinity... but you could not live with your married sister, or your brother, instead of coming alone to London?"

"Good lord, no. My sister is very dear to me, but I think if I stayed with newly-weds for longer than the briefest visit, they would soon hate the very sight of me and wish me gone with the same fervor Mrs. Smith reserves for the mice in her walls."

"Indeed?"

"Oh, I am fully aware of what some folk consider my shortcomings and I try to ameliorate the damage whenever possible, but I cannot change completely, can I? For then I would not be myself. It would be false."

"Pleased with yourself then, are you?"

"I would prefer people to like me for the way I truly am and cannot help but be, rather than for them to like a person I merely pretend to emulate. Therefore to remain a fond thought in the mind of my sister, and to have her always pleased to see me with an embrace of warm affection, some distance and time apart is for the best, I find."

Her features were hidden in the shadows, but her voice was softly pleasing. Not the shrill chatter with which most women cursed his ears. So he listened, in a way that he never usually did, and every word sank in, resonating deeply, as if the sound, if not the words themselves, addressed his very soul.

What a peculiar creature she was.

Again, he saw himself crossing Mrs. Marvington's threshold, carelessly tossing a hat in this young woman's direction and her hands dropping it. Her head bent and the brown ribbon with a moth hole. Now she worked for him. All this time she'd been close, yet he had very nearly missed her entirely.

"As for my brother," she continued, "he barely has room for the wife and children under his roof and I would be an unwanted mouth to feed. So I chose adventure."

"And now, of course, you are engaged to Mr. Darkwaters, the great explorer of Basingstoke."

"Oh." She paused. "Precisely. The great explorer."

"Does he not object to his fiancée working in a shop?"

"He can object all he likes. I am not his property."

"Yet."

"Is that how you see marriage then, sir? As the acquisition of property?"

"I believe that is how most of the world views marriage, madam."

"I see." Her eyes glittered across the distance as she eyed him with that lively bemusement. "I had better make the most of my adventures first then, before I am bought and paid for."

"I pity poor Mr. Darkwaters."

Now that they were out in the countryside with no rooftops, chimneys or spires in its way, the moon was bright and full, its glow obscured only occasionally by a rattling tree limb. With a soft silvery brush that celestial light painted the side of her face as she looked across at him and said solemnly, "I am taking you in, Mr. Deverell, piece by piece. So that I shall remember *this* adventure forever. And when I am old I shall entertain others with the story of how I once traveled into Cornwall with a Deverell, entirely unchaperoned. I daresay they will never believe me."

Adventure? He rubbed his knee. That's what she thought of this journey? Again, a bright outlook that was bound for disappointment.

She was an innocent young woman full of life, laughter and good will. Compared to her, what was he? One of the seven deadly sins.

He looked down and thought that he should have provided a hot brick. Although hidden somewhere in the darkness, her feet must be cold. Unlike most women, she made no complaint.

What would she say, if he asked her? *At least I have feet, even if I cannot feel them at present. Tra-la-la-lala. La-la-la-la.*

He shook his head. Such a woman, always uplifted no matter what the circumstances, would be exhausting company for long. Even that fact she readily and cheerily admitted, when speaking of her siblings and the desire to keep their favor by staying away.

"You frown, sir," she said. "I sense it even though your features are shrouded in darkness."

"A young girl like yourself would be safer in a place like Widecombe with your aunt, than in London, living in a boarding house with strangers. Or serving as companion to some other...woman."

Again, he thought, he really should pay greater attention to the women he hired— or Shepherd hired for him. He'd never given much thought to them before. It had been one of Dockery's bright ideas to employ females in the shop as well as males. "*They'll add a little cheer and color to the place,*" he'd said.

Jacob was an enthusiastic appreciator of ladies. And he would like this one, no doubt.

"But why should my aunt shoulder the expense of my upkeep?" Miss Follyot was saying. "Why should the burden fall to her? As the widow of a vicar, she has limited means herself, and if I found nowhere else to go, she would feel obliged to stretch her little budget and take me in. I could not bear to be such a burden. In any case, Widecombe is a village much like Little Marshes, and after my father died I wanted to see more of the world, meet different people, expand my knowledge and experiences. I didn't want to be stifled. That is what you mean by safer, is it not?"

"I meant *safer*, madam, which is the word I used. I never say what I do not mean."

"But safer, as in— the bird is *safer* in its cage. Or the horse is *safer* with its blinkers on."

"Forgive me, madam. I do not know why I made the observation," he muttered. "I should have kept my thoughts to myself. What you do is of no concern to me. It is wholly a matter for Mr. Dullwaters to trouble himself over."

"Darkwinters!"

"Ah, that's the fellow!" Not that he believed any of that nonsense for a moment.

And how did he know she fibbed about a fiancé?

Because no man in his right mind would leave this intriguing young woman to make her way to

Cornwall in the questionable guardianship of J.P. Deverell. Unchaperoned, as she pointed out. He was surprised, in fact, that her aunt allowed it. His own mother, naturally, thought nothing amiss with it, seeing her son as incapable of wrong-doing. Or pretending not to see it. But then his mother was a unique woman, capable of tolerating his father's scandalous history, so perhaps she easily overlooked her son's faults likewise. As for the young woman's aunt—well, her relatives had once allowed her to take up the post as companion to a notorious divorcee so perhaps they were all fairly naive.

Anne Follyot clearly conjured up the fantasy of a fiancé to reassure J.P. of her disinterest in any potential romance, shielding herself with a make-believe gentleman. He was not, in any way, fooled.

A young lady running wild in the world, making her own choices and "expanding" her experiences with no male to guide her, ought to be a frightening prospect indeed. An unwed woman left on her own to work for a man who never showed his face to the world? Were they all mad to let her do it?

"What does Mr. J.P. Deverell do with his leisure hours away from the office of business? If he will not tell me of his work, perhaps he will talk of his hobbies?"

More prying.

He rubbed his palms on his thighs again, feeling as if she interviewed him for a post. "He has none. He sleeps, he rises, he goes to work. At the end of the day he goes to bed." Unless he stayed all night on the couch by the fire in his office, as he often did. "What else is he meant to do?"

"And where is his home?"

"I keep... two rooms above a shop. It is quite sufficient. I take my meals out."

"Above a shop? How strange! I imagined you would live in a fine, stately house near a park."

"There is naught fine and stately about me."

"No. I see that now. My illusions are shattered."

He glowered at her, although she would not see his expression.

"To go from the wildly beautiful Roscarrock island to rooms above a shop seems very sad!" she said.

"I do own a pleasant house in Arlington Street," he admitted churlishly, not wanting her sympathy. Perhaps even wanting to impress her a little. "I lease it to a retired Admiral, as it is too large for me." There were actually a number of properties he had purchased around town and all leased to good families now. He took quiet pride in buying old buildings that had seen better days, restoring their former glory and finding people to fill them again. Old houses had a story to tell, but they did so in silence and one had to peel away the layers of grime and rust to read it. That was what he found fascinating and incredibly satisfying, even more so than the financial investment. But he could not be sure that was what she meant by a hobby, so he hesitated to explain all that. He rarely left London to spend time in the country, so he did not fish, hunt or shoot. That was all he could presently think she might have meant by her question.

"I like to invent things." The words bounced out of her, not waiting for his encouragement.

"Things?" Bemused, he studied her shadow. The bad news continued to fall just like the snow, he thought. Was there no end to this woman's oddities?

"All manner of gadgetry to make life easier. Of course—" she sighed "—some inventions are more successful than others. I once tried to make a machine to curl my sister's hair without papers and it she became entangled in it so severely that her hair had to be cut off to an inch all over. She still talks of it today, although that was a great many years ago and really one would think she has other matters to dwell upon with a husband and house to manage now. Hair does grow back, for goodness sake, as I assured her at the time. But great discoveries are made through trial and error, are they not? I have yet to find the idea that will make my fortune, but I do not intend to give up."

He was more fascinated by her than he cared to be. "No doubt the world awaits with baited breath, Miss Follyot."

"I like to think so. My father used to say that he was sure I'd amount to something one day."

That optimism explained her own, he thought drily.

Chapter Six

"What a pity you needed me as an excuse to go home for Christmas," she said, taking the conversation off in yet another circle, with barely a pause for breath. "Your family must miss you at home if you never visit."

"I am thirty, madam, not a boy. When a man reaches a certain age in life he ought to make his own home." Then he thought of what she had said before. "As for my family, perhaps, like you, I know how absence makes the heart fonder."

"Yes, but...it *is* Christmas."

He groaned. "This again?"

"All I can say, sir, is that I may not be a little girl anymore, just as you are not a boy, but I wish *my* father were still alive so that I could visit him for Christmas. As much as I am glad to have adventures—" She sniffed. "I do not think we are ever too old to go home for Christmas. If we still have a home." She swallowed. "With a parent in it."

Oh, lord. Were those tears glistening in her eyes?

"If he were still alive, I would be at home in Little Marshes, looking after my father,"

she managed, her voice hoarse, fingers scrambling for something in the dark. "I wouldn't be bothering you now."

He cleared his throat, scowled, irritably flicked his handkerchief into her grasp and then crossed his arms. "I'm sure you'd be bothering somebody. It might as well be me."

"Yes. I daresay." She blew her nose soundly on his handkerchief and then stared out at the moonlit snow again. But he could see her lips trembling as she held back her sobs. "My brother used to laugh that I would never find anybody outside Little Marshes to tolerate me, but that at least our father would have somebody to look after him in his dotage. Well, what am I to do now, but annoy strangers?"

He suspected he ought to say something kind at this pause, but she did not leave a space long enough and he had barely opened his mouth before she added a swift,

"Save your breath to cool your pudding, sir. No need to be conciliatory. I know I am an irritant to most people."

"While I am a cad who deserves the punishment of your company."

There was a pause and then, "Quite."

"Who else but me— in the absence of the distinguished Mr. Darkwinters of Basingstoke— should suffer the discomfort and inconvenience of your company?"

"Hmm."

"I'm the rudest man most folk have ever met, so I'm told, and I'm sure I have confirmed it for you now."

"Yes."

He unfolded his arms. "But I suppose, although this situation is far from ideal for either of us— Miss Follyot the Nuisance and Deverell the Discourteous— we'll just have to make the most of it."

"Yes." She sniffed.

"After all, did you not say this was an adventure?"

Another sigh, wistful.

"By which I assume you referred to the recklessness of travel in winter. Riding out into the blinding snow. Possibly ending our days buried in a snowdrift. Stranded. Our toes rotted off with frostbite. Other parts frozen solid. We must make the most of it all. Because this is the very modern Miss Follyot's glorious adventure."

She turned her head to look at him again, but cautiously this time. Moonlight framed her bonnet. "Do you seek to cheer me, Mr. Deverell?"

Did he? Why on earth did he care? "Such a thing does not have the air of me about it."

When she leaned forward into a silvery shaft of light, he saw that she squinted, her lips pressed tightly together as she considered him carefully.

"I suppose I simply hate to see women cry," he added, churlish. "It makes a red, damp, unsightly mess of their faces, and I do not want to look at you in that state for the next few days. So you see it was for selfish reasons. I am, after all, a blackguard and worse."

Then she laughed. It came out of her on a wave like a sneeze, or a riot of hiccups. It very nearly made him smile too. She kept trying to stop it, but that only seemed to cause another wave, until he was no longer certain whether she was sobbing or laughing.

"Miss Follyot," he muttered, "take a breath, before you explode into a thousand soggy little pieces all over my carriage and have to be scraped off."

She wiped her eyes with his handkerchief. "I...I am sorry, sir. Forgive me."

"I doubt it can be helped entirely. Women are often unduly moist. But do have a care for my upholstery. I fear it's too late for my handkerchief."

She nodded, making a visible effort to speak through that strange mixture of laughter and tears. "I'm afraid, I know where I saw you before, Mr. Deverell."

"At a miserable vicarage party a thousand years ago. I know." *Please do not remember Mrs. Marvington's suite and the thrown hat.* It would not usually bother him what any woman thought of his behavior, but with her it did. For some dreadful reason.

"No, Mr. Deverell. It was today."

He blinked. "Today? Surely not."

"Was it Bond Street, sir, where you fell over that trunk?"

"Yes. I believe so. Why?"

"Oh, good lord! Then it *was* my trunk you fell over, sir."

"Yours? You don't say."

"I had just collected it from Finnigans, where they mended the old thing for me, and I was delayed talking to Mrs. Morgan on the way out— her daughter, Mary, has just had a new baby, such a dear little plump thing with golden curls, rosy cheeks, two darling little dimples and the largest blue—"

"The trunk, Miss Follyot! Explanation, if you please, before I am old and grey."

"Well, as I stood upon the stairs, I did not know that my trunk protruded into the street. It must have slid down onto the pavement somehow. I heard a tremendous clamor suddenly and turned to find a man...down on the ground and cursing. Before I could offer any assistance or apology, he had stormed off in a state of embarrassment, it seemed. It was soon gone from my mind in all the excitement of preparing for my journey. But," she sighed and blew her nose again, "it was you. I see that now. There is an unmistakable disgruntled beastliness about you."

He leaned back, one hand on his thigh, the other arm resting along the back of his seat. "You are brave to admit yourself responsible for my injury."

"Of course, I must own up to it," she said, sounding surprised.

"Even if I toss you out into the snow as a consequence?"

She sniffed. "I decided you wouldn't do that. You were too kind when you thought I wept just now."

"You *were* weeping, for a moment."

"Yes. For a moment. But I do not like to be maudlin about my father. He wouldn't want me to be. It's just...well..."

"Christmas?"

She nodded.

"It has a lot to answer for," he said gruffly.

Miss Follyot seemed to be blushing very slightly, a pinker color tinting that eager, moonlit face. "I am not particularly brave, sir. I knew it was my trunk you fell over as soon as you mentioned how the accident happened. I dare not own up to my part at first, only after you were kind enough to try and make me smile."

He shook his head slowly. "Tsk, tsk!" Concealment of anything, he mused, was probably beyond her for long. It was a delightful change, once he got over the shock of it.

"Now perhaps you will allow me to be concerned about your knee and not fear that I hope for a romantic attachment. I am responsible for the accident. I am guilty."

"Besides, you have no need to bait your romantic hook, for you have Mr. Claiborne Arbuthnot Darkwinters. The third."

She nodded, looking down.

He finally allowed a little smile. "But you really did not have to confess that it was your trunk that attacked me on Bond Street, Miss Follyot."

She adjusted the holly sprig which drooped from her moth-eaten hat ribbon. "I would have felt terribly guilty, if I didn't. My father always said that the best way to the root to a problem is to be honest. He always knew what I had done, sometimes even before I did. He read my face, he said. It is an awful thing to have a face so easily read."

About to make a confession of his own, he banked it. Instead, he let her chatter away again, the grief over her father swept away. For now. As he knew from his own experience of losing a dear friend, such sadness always came back, like the tide. But it did not come and go with the same regularity. One never knew when it might return, creeping in through any tiny crack in one's thoughts, so preparation and protection against its power were impossible.

The fact was, J.P. had already known it was her trunk that attacked him. He'd known it from the moment he lifted the shabby thing onto his shoulder. The familiarity of proximity. Plus the dent in the lid which was about the same size as his fist.

He looked at her and wondered why there was nobody else to take her to the aunt in Widecombe; why that duty had fallen to him. There may not be a Basingstoke explorer, but there ought to be somebody. Of some sort. Somewhere.

Finally she paused for a breath and to clean off the window again with her gloved palm.

"I should have provided a warm brick for your feet, Miss Follyot," he said, the words sounding awkward and not like him at all. "I'm sorry." He cleared his throat again. "They must be cold."

"'Tis fortunate then, that I did not rely upon your gallantry. I used my own initiative," she replied cheerfully, lifting her foot slightly between them to show what was, possibly, the ugliest boot he'd ever seen and surely too large for her feet. "I came well prepared for travel in winter." He caught a glimpse of scarlet wool over the top of the scuffed, thick leather, before she set her foot down again. "They're not pretty, but what they lack in looks they make up for in warmth and practicality. As a child in the countryside, following my father about on his rounds, I discovered the importance of staying warm and dry. I learned to knit by making socks like these for inside his boots. They have an outer coat of oil-cloth sewn in to keep the damp out, should puddle-water creep through the soles. I invented the idea myself and hope one day that Mr. Lockreedy might be persuaded to sell them in his emporium."

"I'm sure something like that already exists, Miss Follyot."

"Oh." She sounded crestfallen. "Do you think so?"

"One would have to investigate the existence of a patent," he muttered. "If there is some unique factor involved...then you might have a worthy idea. The fees for obtaining a patent are a third of what they once were, the process much less complex, of course. I could help—" He stopped there, certain she could have no interest in the dry facts of law. Her hopes and dreams were not his business either. Miss Anne Follyot was both a calamity and a conundrum. And he should be thankful that she was not his concern.

Or was she?

The woman worked for him. That made her a responsibility to some extent, he supposed. A responsibility he had not known he had until tonight. Had never thought about.

Now she studied him even more intently, as if those handful of ventured words had turned a key and opened a door. "How did it happen that you tripped over my trunk? Did you not see it there?"

"Of course I saw it. I fell over it deliberately to injure myself."

"I mean to say, it is not a small item. I suppose you were distracted by something else."

How *had* he fallen over her trunk? It was not like him to be inattentive in the street. He may look as if he stared blankly and directly ahead as he walked, because he did not like to make eye contact with anybody and thus be obliged to acknowledge them, but he was always aware of whatever happened around him. Very little ever escaped his notice. Today something else must have preyed upon his mind.

Something had kept him from seeing her trunk, or her.

And then he fell.

He thought of it now, as if it happened to somebody else and he watched from the other side of Bond Street.

Miss Follyot must have been a few feet away, gossiping— talking, undoubtedly— and with her back turned. What was J.P. doing then? Scowling at the dull, heavy sky as snow threatened.

Before he slipped, he saw a boy slide on a patch of ice and spill a paper cone of hot chestnuts. He had shaken his head and then thought of Jacob Dockery, who loved hot chestnuts. Particularly the sport of aiming them at the back of J.P.'s head.

Yes, that was what he had been doing: missing his old friend.

"I merely asked about your leg to be polite," Miss Anne Follyot had exclaimed. *"It would have been odd if I avoided the subject, I suppose. But I can assure you, I do not care if it falls off altogether."*

An amusingly impudent comment, made even more so by the newly disclosed fact that she had known her trunk was at fault.

Miss Follyot now speculated aloud on all the things that might have distracted him in the street, from poodles to pretty ladies, toothache to sugar plums. Even unicorns. The more unlikely and preposterous the better. She amused herself with this, so he let her go on interrupted. At least she was no longer on the verge of weeping.

He was struck then by how much she reminded him of Jacob Dockery. Their cheerful personalities and the way they teased him were strikingly similar. The miles had trotted by at a brisk pace in her company.

J.P. missed his friend. He had not realized until that moment— had not let himself think of it— how very much he missed that friendship: the ease of it, the trust and confidences they shared, and the ability Jacob had to make him laugh at himself.

Nobody else ever dared try. Or cared to.

Yes, grief could overtake a person quite suddenly, when they were least expecting it. The hollow ache in one's heart was something that could not be controlled or managed.

Emotions. He shuddered. How he hated feeling them. It ought to be possible to stop them.

"When you saw that a gentleman had tripped over your trunk, Miss Follyot, did you see the old woman who helped him up?"

She frowned. "No. Only you. The back of you, at least, limping away and cursing the pavement."

"Steady there, young man! Look where you're going, before 'tis too late."

It occurred to him then that perhaps it wasn't that he fell today because something prevented him from seeing her trunk; instead something or someone had used that trunk to try and make him see *her* there. Finally.

Chapter Seven

Over the past two decades, since the advance of the railway and thus the weakening demand for travel by carriage, several old coaching inns on the route west from London had been torn down. J.P. marked their loss in silence, solemnly remembering each one where it once stood with lanterns in the windows and clumps of horse dung dotted about the yard— places of rowdy comings and goings, including his own, since he turned eight and was first sent off with the mail coach to boarding school.

The past was such a strange creature, distorted and foggy, and he did not like to visit there often. Tonight, however, marking all the changes along this road, he ventured back through a door and let his mind wander.

As a boy he had been fascinated by these coaching inns and the variety of people surrounding them; the dashing about and piles of luggage; the sense of urgency and excitement. Then he grew up, of course, and as he sprouted taller he found himself being noticed and stared at, his own purpose questioned, the scandals of his family swirling about him in whispers, like autumn wind carrying dead leaves. That was when he stopped showing interest in other passengers and simply stared ahead, hoping to arrive at his destination as quickly as possible.

Where did all that childhood curiosity go? Why did the adventure of the journey vanish with it? As an adult he knew too much about the complications and entanglements in other people's lives— the ugly tawdriness too. That put a stop to boyish innocence and likewise curiosity.

Miss Follyot did not appear to have lost hers, however. She had a thirst for discovery.

"When was the last time you went home to see your family?" she inquired.

He told her that he could not remember. He supposed it was four years ago, or thereabouts, but answering her questions with too much information usually led to more questions on the same vein, so he kept his replies short. Although it was futile to hope she'd run out of questions, at least her subject would change.

"I have not been to Cornwall since I was a child," she said. "Apparently that vicarage tea party at Porthwellen took place during a visit there to my aunt and uncle when I was only five, but I have vague memories of the coast as a beautiful place. You were very lucky to have spent a childhood there by the sea."

A lucky childhood? Was it? He remembered a great deal of time alone studying his school books, because his siblings were so much older— the youngest of them being fifteen years older than J.P. He had nieces and nephews older than himself.

"I never expected to marry a second time," his father had said to him once. "Certainly I thought I had enough children to manage. Then along came your mama one day and... well...all that changed. It does, you know, when you find yourself struck by an angel."

His father was a man who did not believe in the need to explain himself, so that much elucidation from his lips was unusual. But it was not particularly comforting for J.P. that his existence was the one thing that must be accounted for.

"This is John Paul. The child of my second marriage," he'd heard his father say by way of introduction. "A surprise gift to me when I thought I was done raising children, which proves that man has no control over his future. He should not even attempt to predict it."

Sometimes J.P. felt a distance between himself and his father. What caused it he had no idea, but there was a chasm of some depth and space. It was even more puzzling because he knew his parents' marriage was a love match. Still was, even after all these years. Yet his father reacted cautiously around him, uneasy, leaving things to his mother.

"He's so clever," he'd heard his father marvel out loud once. "So wise beyond his years. He must take after you, Olivia."

His father, born a foundling, never had the benefit of a formal education and was mostly self taught. It seemed as if he was almost intimidated by his youngest son's mind. It must be a strange thing indeed for a tough-skinned scrapper like True Deverell to be unsettled by anything, least of all his own flesh and blood. But J.P. wished he could bridge that gap between them, somehow. Make his father see how important he was to him. How he would always look up to him.

If only he could express himself as easily as Miss Follyot chattered about the love she felt for her own father.

"You seem lost in thought, Mr. Deverell," said his traveling companion suddenly. "I hope it is not unhappy thought or that I am to blame for it with my nosiness."

"I was merely thinking how much I —how much has changed along this road in recent times."

But as their journey wound onward and they traveled farther from London, the scenery began to look more as he remembered, preserved as it had been for several hundred years, unmolested by new industry and its demands. As the horses took them by milestones in the snow, white-clad, thatched rooftops and frosty Tudor beams reappeared through his carriage window. It was like revisiting the past. J.P. liked to know that not everything must be pushed aside to make way for the future. Jacob Dockery used to say his friend was an old-fashioned gentleman at heart. As if there was something wrong with that.

They turned into a coaching inn for supper and a change of horses.

"Should we pretend that I am your niece?" she whispered, her breath shivering with excitement.

He frowned. "Why on earth would that be necessary?"

"People might talk."

"Your aunt and my mother did not seem perturbed by the possibility when she entrusted you to my hands."

"Or you to mine." She laughed.

"Yes, well, we've established that you're not trying to seduce me."

"I would not know where to begin."

Which made her, somehow, even more interesting. He sighed, head bowed.

"What's the matter?" she asked.

He shook his head. "Absolutely nothing or too many things to mention." He had not yet decided.

There was only one private dining room and that was taken, so they were obliged to eat in the public tavern, where they ordered "pie", an object thus called with no other explanation or description given for its contents, and no alternative offered. J.P. ate very little, finding himself thirsty rather than hungry, in any case.

In the light of oil lamps, able to study his companion's face properly for the first time, he was surprised to find her not at all plain, as he'd suspected she might be from his mother's letter. Perhaps it was the fact that he had listened to her chatter for several hours before he even saw her face, but it was pleasant to look upon, like that of an old friend one had missed and looked forward to seeing again. He kept looking at it to find fault, but the pleasure did not fade.

How strange. It was most unlike J.P. to get to know a woman. Any woman. He generally had no desire to know them outside a bed. Yet this one he had conversed with for hours before her face was fully revealed to him.

Still he had no memory of meeting her when they were children. Why his mother thought he might remember her was anybody's guess.

"Do you suppose there are many folk here embarked upon illicit affairs?" she whispered across the small table. "Eloping to be married, or running away from spouses? In disguise and with secret love letters and lucky rabbit's feet sewn into their petticoats?"

"Do you read a lot of novels, Miss Follyot?"

"An inordinate amount according to almost everybody," she admitted proudly. "But they are much more interesting than the newspaper and usually more uplifting. I suppose novels are not important enough for you to read."

He picked up the printed tally left on the table by the barman, inspecting the cost of this doubtful "pie" and watery ale. The quality of the food had not changed in all these years, but the prices had.

"What do you like to read then?" she demanded. "Only items of business and political pamphlets? And bills?"

"I read what must be read for information. I do not read for entertainment. I seldom have the luxury of time to waste on worthless pursuit."

"You poor, poor, dear thing."

Why did she keep doing that— gazing at him with big, sad eyes? Making him feel as if his existence lacked something. This was a woman who lived in a shabby boarding house, worked for a little wage in a shop, and had nothing to her name but a dented trunk of garments she herself disdained as worthless. Her future was in doubt, her family apparently in denial— or else desperate enough to throw her in his direction. Yet she looked with pity at him.

He put the bill down again. "I am quite content in my work and life. Spare your sympathy."

"But you miss out on a vast amount of happiness."

"Because I have no time to read stories of make-believe? What good would they do me?"

"It might give you something else to think about and exercise your mind in new ways."

"My mind does not require exercise."

She sighed. "Yes, I'm sure it's a great big, stubborn muscle already."

"I beg your pardon?"

Hastily she continued, "Did you never like stories, even as a child?"

"Miss Follyot, I can scarce recall *being* a child."

"Well, I think that's dreadful. Yet, I know—" She held up her hands, both spread before him, palms in his face. "You do not want my pity. Your narrow mind is not my concern, just as my reckless independence is not yours. So I must be silent on the matter, being a modern girl."

"Silent? Surely that's impossible. Your tongue is a stubborn muscle, like my mind."

She shook her head and dug a fork into her pie. "I do like to read the *Exchange and Mart*," she said. "All the bric-a-brac people want to sell and buy. It makes one wonder about their lives— how they came into the possession of so many stamps, old magazines or flower pots that they no longer want, or what happened that makes them give away a doll's china tea set. Once there was an advertisement by a man seeking ladies' cast-off silk drawers. Now, what do you suppose he wanted them for?"

He coughed as a piece of tough pastry went down the wrong pipe. "The mind is...left to wonder, indeed. Some people simply collect detritus, Miss Follyot."

"But there is always a story behind it, don't you think?"

"Perhaps one that is best not known in some cases. Eat your pie, before it gets cold. At least warm it is partially edible."

And while eating, she could not talk as much. He might have time then to consider what was happening to him. To stop his world from spinning recklessly.

"Are you blushing, Mr. Deverell?"

"It is hot in here."

"You're blushing about the silk drawers."

"I most certainly am not."

"No. I suppose you've seen a great many pairs. They are nothing to a rogue of your experience."

He refused to grace that with an answer.

But the silence began to feel uncomfortable. He must be getting accustomed to her noise, he mused.

"You did not send him yours, I hope," he muttered crossly.

"What sort of woman do you think I am? And do you think it's proper to ask me such a question?"

But he caught the gleam of something naughty in her eyes, before she looked down at her plate.

He changed the subject back to safer territory. Books. Ah, yes. "As a matter of fact, I read a book by Mr. Charles Dickens recently. Somebody left it on my desk in the office."

"Somebody?"

"None would confess to it, but I have my suspicions." They tried to tell him that he was in danger of turning into Ebenezer Scrooge, of course. Since he had no time to read the end of the book, he saw no reason why this comparison should be a bad thing.

He took the fob watch from his waistcoat and examined it.

"If you have no objection, Miss Follyot, I would like to get as far as The George and Dragon near Farnborough tonight. It is a very respectable place, and I know the inn-keeper. He will provide comfortable, secure rooms and the stables are excellent— better than these here. We should make haste before the snow gets much deeper tonight."

"As you wish. I, Anne Follyot of Little Marshes and a lot of brown, put myself in your hands, Deverell. You have more familiarity with the road than I do."

"Yes." Begrudgingly he added, "I traveled it many times, to and from boarding school as a boy and then as a young man at university." It was not like him to tell a stranger even this much.

"How fortunate you were to go to school. My brother was sent away also to boarding school, but he did not get along well there and came home more than he was away. My sister and I had to teach ourselves if we wanted to learn. It was most unfair, really, for my brother Wilfred, despite his opportunities, was always lazy and— it must be said, I think he was proud of it— rather thick-headed. He had no interest in learning or following our father's footsteps. Had our fortunes permitted it, he would have been a gentleman of leisure, no doubt. On the other hand, I would gladly have trained as a veterinarian, like my father, but I am the wrong gender. Such study is not fitting for a woman, my parents agreed. Still, early in the morning in lambing season, I was the one who went out with my father to help in the cold snow while it was still dark out, trudging along in his footsteps, getting happily filthy."

Her face shone as she spoke of these memories.

"In your special, water-proof, knitted socks," he said.

"Yes." Then her shoulders lowered and she looked down at the crumbs of her pie. "I was always useful rather than ornamental. I don't suppose that is any surprise to you."

He said nothing.

"After my mother died, my only purpose was to manage the house and look after my father. From the time I was ten, I looked after everybody, just as she once did. I tried to give up thinking of myself, but sometimes my father would come home with a little treat, something just for me, to say he understood and valued how hard I tried. A bundle of wildflowers or a button he found. My father always knew what I would like, without a word being said. Our souls were very close. That is love, I suppose, a connection that needs no words. It is very hard when that is gone. To find oneself suddenly alone."

J.P. wondered why she told him all this. She flung open the doors of her life to him, a virtual stranger, without a care. Innocence again, he thought glumly. Naiveté. It was not something he had known in many women. Respectable, polite, honest women did not approach him, and he would never approach anybody. His past experiences, therefore, were with women of a certain kind. Much to Jacob Dockery's amusement and his own mother's frustration.

Other women would throw their silk drawers at him readily enough, but they would not bare their souls.

He glanced over at the tavern door as it swung open with a gust of snowy wind and let in a ghost of his past.

* * * *

December 1864

His heels slid across the wet stone floor as a stout wind thrust his young self through the door, along with a scattering of snow, a glittering trail at his feet.

"Ale and plenty of it," exclaimed Jacob, falling through the door after him. "That must be the first order of business."

He nodded, too cold to speak, his lips stuck to his scarf.

They were on their way to Roscarrock, Jacob coming along as his guest for the very first time. It had taken J.P. some time to pluck up the resolve to invite him, but then it turned out that Jacob had nowhere else to go that year and would have had to stay at school.

"You had better come with me then, I suppose," J.P. had muttered warily. He had always tried to keep friends separate from his family, so that he had something of his own.

"Excellent!" Jacob had beamed. "I shall finally meet the infamous True Deverell and see what all the fuss is about."

"A storm in a teacup, my mother has always said. I hope you won't be disappointed."

"I shall be fascinated, old chap. And just as pleased to meet your mama. To meet any of your family, since you are so loath to speak of them. I almost wondered if they truly exist."

They ordered two pints of the "best" ale.

"We have precisely one hour before the next mail coach leaves," he had remarked after checking his fob watch. "I would not imbibe too much, if I were you, Dockery. I do not care to lift you bodily into the carriage."

"How lucky I am to have you watching over me, Deverell. To see that I am on my best behavior." But he would do as he pleased anyway, of course, maintaining a charming smile the entire time, which made it quite impossible to be angry. "Do you never just simply enjoy life and abandon yourself to fate?"

"No."

A moment later the door opened again and a woman in a grey, hooded cloak entered the tavern. He would not have noticed her if Dockery did not draw his attention to the new arrival and even then he looked only once before turning his back. It was the wife of their science tutor and house master at school, a woman in her thirties, well-maintained and verging on what his mother would call "brassy".

All the boys at school speculated on the private life of Mrs. Randall, for there were rumors of her taste for younger men and Mr. Randall's well-turned blind eye. All the boys, that is, except J.P., who never gossiped about anybody. His misbehavior was achieved quietly, in the dark.

"What can she be doing this far from London?" Jacob had recognized her at once. "And all alone it seems. How very curious."

J.P. said nothing. Sometimes he thought his friend knew, although Jacob never spoke of it directly. He hinted, or threw out baited hooks with which to reel in a confession, but J.P. was too careful and discreet to be caught.

"There must be a woman somewhere that has caught your eye," Jacob would exclaim. "I know you like your studies, but even you must need some recreation with the female sex. You're a Deverell, for pity's sake!"

J.P. would merely smile. "You worry about your own females, Dockery." There were, after all, many of them, and Jacob was an inept juggler.

Mrs. Randall came into J.P.'s life when he was seventeen and inquisitive— wondering what all the fuss was about. She pursued him, apparently seeing in the tall, quiet, solemn young man something alluring. Something different, he supposed. That was the only way he could explain her attraction to him. They did not speak a great deal, having nothing in common. He really knew very little about her, or she about him. It was better that way, he quickly decided.

Their affair lasted a few months that winter, and J.P. saw it as a necessary schooling. She, apparently, thought it was more than that.

She would have followed him all the way to Cornwall when he went home for Christmas, but when she entered the door of that tavern and found Jacob Dockery in his company, she was obliged to turn around and go back through the snow to her husband. J.P. had neglected to tell her he was taking a guest, but then he had not expected her to follow him. It had not occurred to him that she would even get the thought into her head. But apparently, she took their affair far more seriously than he did.

While he was home at Roscarrock that Christmas, he worried about Mrs. Randall and her odd behavior. By the time he returned to school in the new year, he had decided to end it. In her absence he had come to his senses, realized that he liked having time to himself again. The distance between them had cleared his head and refocused his thoughts. But then he found that a goodbye was not necessary. Her husband had been given a new posting in another school and she had gone with him. J.P. was able to concentrate fully on his final exams for university.

Now, when he thought back to his stolen afternoons with Mrs. Randall, he considered her as another tutor from his school days. She was certainly diligent in her teaching, and thorough. He had given her little in return; had never even bought her flowers. Perhaps he should have taken more time to know her and been concerned. After all, she must have been unhappy in her life, to seek comfort from schoolboys. But he had thought only of himself and set her aside easily, even with relief.

His only excuse could be youth. At seventeen what did he know of anything? What did she expect him to know?

In that moment, all those years ago, when he turned from his ale to follow Jacob Dockery's gaze, and saw her in the door of the tavern— watched her expression turn from gladness to surprise, from desperation and sadness to acceptance— young J.P. had realized two things: that he knew nothing about women, and that Christmas made people do odd things and nurture romantic ideas with no root in reality.

"I hope you are cautious with women, Jean Paul," his father had said quietly to him over the punch bowl. "You are young. Do not get yourself entangled with another man's trouble and strife. It will follow you forever, if you do."

The Randall family's transfer to a new post had not seemed odd at the time. But now J.P. wondered. He thought of Miss Follyot's confession earlier.

"My father always said that the best way to the root to a problem is to be honest. He always knew what I had done,

sometimes even before I did. He read my face, he said. It is an awful thing to have a face so easily read."

True Deverell also had ways of finding the root to a problem, especially when it came to his "litter" of children. Had J.P.'s behavior at home that Christmas caused his father to suspect something amiss? Had he questioned Jacob Dockery about his son's life at school? Something had caused Mr. Randall's sudden removal to another place, his wife with him.

Fathers could work in mysterious ways. Miss Follyot had made him study his own father through new eyes.

"My father always knew what I would like, without a word being said. Our souls were very close. That is love, I suppose, a connection that needs no words."

There were times when J.P. wished his father talked to him more than he did. But perhaps it was not necessary, when the understanding was there without words.

* * * *

More folk had tumbled in through the tavern door, snow-coated and red-nosed, glad to be inside out of the cold, chattering and laughing. There was a woman among them, in her forties with red hair, so bright it must be dyed. For just a moment he imagined it was Mrs. Randall, but it was not, of course.

Did she ever think of him? Did she even remember the grave, bookish seventeen-year-old student she once pursued through the snow?

She was the first ghost of his past to visit that evening. He had a feeling she would not be the last spirit to whom he said goodbye.

Something inside him was changing. He was taking that step forward, prodded by his old friend, even as he looked back over one shoulder. Searching for whatever it was he'd missed.

Chapter Eight

"Mr. Deverell, you were far away! I don't believe you were listening to me at all," Miss Follyot exclaimed.

They were back in the carriage now, rattling across the cobbled yard, lantern light swaying across their faces.

"I confess to being weary," he said. "I have had a long day, and I do not possess your energy, I fear." Who did? He would like to meet the person...or perhaps not. She was quite enough to contend with.

"Then I should hold my tongue and let you sleep."

He very much doubted that was possible. It might do her an injury of some sort.

"I promise not to go through your pockets while your eyes are shut," she added mischievously.

She was brave to tease him; few *men* ever did and women seemed to lose their sense of humor entirely in his presence.

"You would not find much in my pockets, madam. Just enough for the journey, carefully measured out."

"And a fob watch. I saw you consult it several times at the tavern. Or is there a picture of your sweetheart inside? A lock of hair?"

"I do not have sweethearts, Miss Follyot."

"Not even one?" She gave an arch smile.

Had she remembered him now as one of Mrs. Marvington's lovers? There was something smug in her expression. Well, he certainly did not consider that lady a "sweetheart", so he replied smoothly,

"No." With a quirk of his eyebrow he dared her to argue.

Her eyes narrowed. "A portrait of your mama then?"

"My mother would never agree to have her likeness taken, even for my father. She says she would not want people looking at her while she is unaware of their perusal."

They pulled away from the lights of the tavern and back onto the road. He heard her tapping her wicker basket again in the darkness, while she considered this. "Your mother sounds most interesting. My aunt speaks fondly of her friendship."

"She is a very intelligent woman, surprisingly sane. For my family." What would she make of Miss Anne Follyot, he wondered, watching his passenger's shadowy silhouette through wary eyes.

What a funny, fearless creature she is.

Yes, he imagined his mother whispering in his ear. She would find Miss Follyot amusing, without a doubt. As he did.

J.P. had always been grateful for his mother— a family member he could rely upon for common sense. One always knew exactly how she would behave, and that she would be wherever she said she would, when she said she would be there. Very different to other members of his family.

She had once claimed that she resisted posing for a portrait because she feared his father might be home much less if he had a picture to look at rather than the real woman. His father's attention was a challenge to pin down; they both knew that, but J.P. was certain she merely teased. For when True

Deverell looked at his wife there was no mistaking the heat of his affection for her, and vice versa.

J.P. used to hope he would one day find a woman that looked at him that way, but as time passed it seemed less and less likely. By now he had given up on the idea as a youthful folly. Not everybody could find love, or was worthy of it. And he had his work, at which he was successful. That was, perhaps, what he was meant to do with his life. Most women were like children, difficult and time consuming. Hell's imps in tiny shoes that were always a great expense.

Yes, he could think of many reasons why it was better to be alone than to marry.

After all, look at everything his father went through before he found his second wife, and J.P.'s mother had survived three husbands before she walked into True Deverell's life.

Let other people in and one's world became complicated.

He shut his eyes.

Miss Follyot could have all the adventure she wanted; she needn't think he was the least little bit interested in joining her.

* * * *

Anne decided to let him have his thoughts without further interruption. The excitement of their journey still bubbled through her— not contained by his stern manner— but she must contain herself and let him rest. He looked tired and frayed.

Her brother used to say she could drive an honest man insane with her chatter. Poor Mr. J.P.

Deverell, Esq., looked as if he had troubles enough without her disturbing his sleep with her foolish ponderings.

His eyes were shut now, but she was not certain he slept.

Mr. Thursday. Yes, of course she recognized him now, having seen his face in the tavern lamplight. He was Mrs. Marvington's Thursday gentleman. One of that lady's "Seven Sins." How could she not know him, since he— or rather the scent of his shaving soap— had caused her a few skips of the heartbeat during her weeks in Mrs. Marvington's employment?

Oh, she should have held her tongue earlier in the carriage, but it had not occurred to her and how was she to guess he had any connection with the lady, until she saw his face clearly and fully? And took in a deeper, braver breath of that spicy, warm fragrance.

Well, he was not a stupid man; he must have known he was not the lady's only gentleman caller, surely. He had not seemed very upset about Mrs. Marvington's parade of lovers, had barely made a sound. No, he was a man of the world and knew more about such things than she. People of the upper classes conducted their affairs in strange ways, and J.P. Deverell was, according to her landlady, a rake and a seducer.

On a few Thursdays he had passed her in Mrs. Marvington's doorway, coming in as she went out, or vice versa. A brush of a sleeve, a scent of that mysterious spice. She had never dared stare at his face, but averted her gaze demurely. Of all that lady's gentlemen, he was the most interesting— perhaps because he said so little and yet seemed such a great presence. Just that slight, passing contact with him awoke her senses, enlivened her thoughts, startling them into spinning action, her nerves turning like frantic whirligigs that, once in danger of becoming rusted, suddenly found wind to make them turn again.

She had not known his name, of course, or that they'd met once at a vicarage tea party.

How strange that fate should keep moving them together. Like dancers in a ballroom, never quite seeing each other. Until now.

Why now? How had it happened that he finally opened his eyes only to fall head first over her trunk in the street?

The street was icy, perilous. She ought to know, having slipped on it herself recently. Still felt the bruises, although she could not recall exactly when she fell.

For a man of his size and arrogance, it would have been humiliating.

And on a Thursday too. She realized he must have been on his way to visit Mrs. Marvington when her trunk "attacked" him, as he put it.

But before that there was the letter from her aunt, offering such an unlikely escort.

Anne thought about his suspicions regarding her aunt and his mother, but it seemed very unlikely to her. Aunt Follyot was entirely too sensible to contrive such a plan, and Mrs. Deverell must know how well it would be received by her son. He did not need his mother finding women for him. Especially not Anne Follyot, who could be of no interest to such a man.

No, she was certain the two ladies merely put the plan of a shared carriage together for practical reasons without any hope of romance blossoming. After all, two more different people one could rarely find anywhere.

He was dubious of her Mr. Darkwinters, but what did it matter? At least he knew now that she had no designs upon him. None of any sort. Her "fiancé" was a flimsy barrier, like his newspaper— a symbol; something that said, *I am not interested in you,* even when it would not stand up to much force.

She looked out at the snow and hugged her basket of paper-wrapped provisions from Lockreedy & Velder's Universal Emporium, trying to enjoy her great adventure as quietly and prudently as possible. She might never have another.

As the stars twinkled down at her, she thought of her father again.

Oh, papa, if only I could be sophisticated and think of clever things to say. Scintillating conversation of the sort Mr. J.P. Deverell must be accustomed.

But even if she possessed pearls, like those Mrs. Marvington wore around her slender throat, she would not know how to twirl them convincingly without getting her fingers tangled.

Anne imagined her father laughing softly, telling her to be herself. No pearls. No rose madder. No pretend fiancé.

Herself. The irritating creature who had never done anything exciting— really, was not allowed to— and for whom brown was always the best choice? No wonder she tried too hard, talked too much, and couldn't sit still. She was over-compensating for her dreariness.

As she always did. Working hard to please, to be approved of.

"You're a girl," her brother would remind her. "You don't know anything important, and you don't impress anybody by pretending that you do, so you may as well shut up. You are so very annoying, merely standing there. The least you can do is be silent."

Memories of childhood Christmases fluttered and sparkled through her thoughts like candlelight caught upon swaying crystal prisms. She was now far away from Little Marshes and the stone cottage at the foot of a bridge, where she grew up, yet it was all clear in her mind, every detail.

She saw the decorated mantle and the cozy fire with her father's wet boots drying beside it; the chenille tablecloth with the ball fringe, and the upright piano at which she and her siblings thumped out music, of a sort. Her mother had always been busy, the sleeves of her dress rolled back over strong forearms, a pinafore tied over her front, her face pink and moist from the heat of the range as she hummed along.

"Anne, be a dear and set the table."

"Anne, put more coal on the fire. Just one shovel, if you please! And carefully! Don't be wasteful."

"Anne, did you sweep that floor? It looks grubby to me."

"Anne, measure the tea into the pot."

All these duties fell to her, because her sister Lizzie's was too small and either could not reach, or dropped things. Deliberately, Anne sometimes thought. As for Wilfred, he would never be asked to perform such menial tasks. Great things were expected of him and so he must study and be left in peace, his temper tip-toed around, his mood sweetened with toffee and sugar plums.

Anne did not mind her place in the family. She preferred to be busy, like her mother, and to make everybody's life easier. Especially her father's. He worked hard, in all weathers and at all hours, tending the livestock of farms for many miles around. When he came home, if Anne had not gone with him on his rounds, he had plenty of tales to tell. Her tasks all done, for now, she would sit by him, her chin in her hand, and listen to his deep voice and the crackling of the coal fire, until she grew sleepy, her eyes closing.

"Don't pretend you're interested, or that you understand anything he says," her brother had remarked once. "You're a girl. You're stupid. But that's alright, because you don't need a brain."

But Anne was not pretending. Perhaps she *did* hope for her father's approval, but she was also genuinely interested and always curious.

"All you need learn is how to be quiet and just do as you're told without questioning everything," her brother would say.

Wilfred's sneering comments did not concern her, however. She knew he was an unhappy person, insecure in his own skin, who could only feel better by belittling others. The Follyot's humble home in the country was not enough for him and he wanted more, but was not prepared to work for it. He was destined for disappointment, but thanked nobody for warning him.

"Little Marshes is the very end of the earth," he muttered wearily. "Nothing ever happens here."

He would never want to earn a living by getting himself covered in dirt, sweat, blood and worse, like their father, but then he did not fancy earning a living in any manner and seemed to be hoping for a surprise inheritance that would allow him to abandon his studies, take up residence in London, or some other large, fashionable town, and live the leisurely life of a gentleman.

"Of course things happen here," Anne had replied. "There is birth and death and everything in between. But you are not interested in other people."

"And you're too interested in them. You're nosy. You're an irritating person, Anne Follyot," he snapped at her. "You never shut up."

When their mother died, it fell to Anne, at ten years of age, to parcel up her old clothes, hats and boots and take them to the parish charity. The household was, for the next ten years, Anne's to manage as best she could, but she was glad of the occupation to keep sadness at bay. Each Christmas she decorated the house just as their mother always had and cooked the same food, following the old recipes faithfully, even when it meant stacking cushions on a chair and kneeling on it just to stir the pudding mixture properly.

She talked a great deal to fill her days, mostly because nobody else did. Her father was tired and silently grieving when he was not busy; her brother was sulking and ill-tempered when not sleeping or away at university, and Lizzie was too young to say anything sensible. Without Anne the house would have been silent and maudlin.

"You're a good girl, Anne," her father said. "You look after us."

The fire hissed and crackled, the candle-flames danced and the crystals prisms that hung from the lamp shade spun slowly.

"I shall have you to tend me in my dotage, shan't I?"

"Of course, papa." She sat at his feet cutting a chain of figures out of newspaper. There was nowhere else in the world she would rather be at Christmas, or any time of year, and she wanted to make it just the same as it had always been. Otherwise her mother, looking down on the house, would be disappointed.

"Anne will never have anywhere else to go," her brother remarked, scornful. Home from the school he hated, he sought ways to hurt everybody around him, as usual. "So she might as well stay here. Who else would want the chatterbox?"

Later, before she went up to her bed, she heard her father admonish Wilfred for speaking so harshly. She paused behind the door when she heard her name mentioned.

"You are unkind to Anne. She may never find a husband as we have nothing much by way of a dowry to offer and very few prospects in Little Marshes, but there is no call for you to remind her of it."

"Even if she had a thousand pounds and a pretty face, it would be a brave or a stupid cove to put up with her. She makes up stories and tells the most dreadful fibs. If you ask me, she's not all there in the head. It would be as well for her to stay here in this village than to go out into the world and embarrass us."

"Wilfred, you've drunk too much brandy. I shan't tell you again! Now, it's Christmas and our first without your mother. Be kind to your sister. If she has not much to look forward to in her future, then let her have her stories. Her poor prospects are all the more reason for you to be thoughtful and considerate."

She went to her bed that Christmas Eve thinking about what she'd heard. Yes, she made up stories to brighten her own days and to make five-year-old Lizzie fall asleep at night, but there was nothing amiss with her head.

"I worry about Anne," she'd heard her mother say once, before she died. "What will become of her? She's always restless, dreaming out loud and talking to herself."

Well, of course she talked to herself. Nobody else would listen!

She made up stories about her life, "dreaming out loud", because what else was one meant to do with an imagination, but use it?

"Yesterday she stood out in the rain and would not come in," her mother had added with a fretful sigh. "Laughing and dancing in it she was, not a thought about her clothes or catching her death. If anybody passed over the bridge just then they would have thought her fit to be carted off to bedlam."

"Anne will be all right," her father had replied. "She's just different. She marches to her own drum."

"She does not march to any drum. She skips to silence, dances to music nobody else hears. That's the trouble with Anne."

On that Christmas Eve, the first without her mother, Anne went to bed feeling dejected and lost, the future a dark place in her thoughts. Wind blew against her window and the room was cold, but she was too hot to sleep, for Lizzie carried the heat of twenty hot water bottles and always managed to press her sweaty little body against Anne at night. So she pushed her sister with both hands, rolling her over to the other side of the mattress and then sat up, reaching for the box of Lucifer matches. Her candle relit, she climbed out of bed.

"Where are you going?" Lizzie complained sleepily from under the blanket.

"Nowhere. Apparently. According to the men in this family. And according to the women, straight to bedlam." She opened her dresser drawer and fumbled for the little tin she kept tucked away in the back. In here she kept her treasures: a lock of her mother's hair and one of her thimbles; a humorous valentine card from her papa, and a stone she'd found that looked like a rabbit. And there in the bottom of the tin, a white paper angel that somebody once made for her.

She took the angel out carefully and fluffed her skirt. "It's Christmas Eve, and I forgot to take you out. Forgive me."

There— she set the angel atop her dresser— and sighed with contentment. She had felt something was missing, because she was not her usually cheerful self that evening, but now it was better. The snow angel always lifted her spirits, as if it carried her heart on its pretty wings. Such a cleverly made, lovely, delicate thing it was. Nothing like Anne Follyot, who was plain, sturdy and talked too much. But the snow angel did not need suitors, or a fortune; she was perfectly content on her own and beautiful, even though she had no features on her face. Somehow the paper angel made everything better. Looking at her, one could think only good, happy, hopeful thoughts.

Anne was only ten, and she reminded herself of that fact. It was easy to forget with so many duties and responsibilities laid in her lap. But there was a lot of time ahead of her. No need to worry about the future tonight. Her father still needed her and so did Lizzie. So did Wilf, not that he would admit it.

She climbed back into bed, keeping the snow angel in her sights.

"I don't know how you came to be mine," she whispered, "but I'm very glad you're here."

Unlike her mother, the snow angel would not die and leave her. It was within Anne's power to keep her angel safe in that tin, to protect her from the elements, sickness and death. There was little else in life over which she had that power. Having lost one parent while she was young, Anne knew that bad things happened, no matter how hard one prayed for good. But she could save her angel. And in return the angel saved her.

It was an unspoken pact.

Even when the candle was once again snuffed out, the snow angel glowed softly with her peculiar, magical form of comfort, absorbing and reflecting moonlight through the window. Soon, Anne did not care about how nobody else would ever want her because she was too bothersome. She would have adventures in her mind and conjure a handsome prince there for her precious snow angel. That would be a far better story than making a prince for herself.

She thought she'd rather have a toad, actually. Toads were delightful and used their eyeballs to swallow. What could be better than that?

The Snow Angel

* * * *

Anne looked across the carriage. Mr. J.P. Deverell seemed to be asleep now, with his arms crossed over his chest, head bowed, the gleam of his wicked eyes hidden. She took a blanket from inside her wicker basket, unfolded it, and placed it cautiously over his knees. She did not dare try tucking it in incase he woke, seized her by the throat and shook her senseless, having forgotten who she was or why she was there.

See? There went her lurid imagination. The one that Wilfred thought made her addled and a few steps shy of the madhouse. Already it was writing stories about her journey, not content with the reality.

Poor Mr. Deverell was not a dragon, a bear or a devil. He was just a man who worked too hard and was so busy that he took no pleasure in life. Something about his sadness made her want to help him. What he needed was a snow angel to save him.

Mrs. Marvington could not have done him much good, for her affections were divided in portions, dealt out meanly and never constant. Her mood had depended on whatever she could get from the man that visited that day, what she expected from him. Tradesmen at Covent Garden market were less mercenary.

The carriage went over a bump and the blanket slid a few inches down his thighs. Well, that wouldn't do. He'd be cold again and soon her blanket would fall upon the floor, which was marked with dirt from their boots. So she hitched to the edge of her seat and very carefully moved the blanket up to his arms. If she could just wedge the fringe somehow between his gloved fingers, it should be prevented from drifting down.

But suddenly they swerved and she tumbled forward into the blanket and his lap. In her surprise, she inhaled the scent of him: leather, tobacco, cognac and exotic spice. There was no time for more than one stolen breath, however, for the beast was awoken and, as one might expect, he roared.

Chapter Nine

"Miss Follyot! What the devil—?" Startled awake, he instinctively put his hands on her waist and then wheezed in agony as she twisted around, stabbing him in the stomach with her elbow. "I told you I had nothing in my pockets. Kindly unhand me, madam."

"I meant only to tuck you in securely," she exclaimed, breathless. "And you're the one handling me, sir."

"*Tuck me in*?" he exclaimed, as if he'd never heard anything so preposterous.

"I thought you must be cold." She showed him the blanket, which she now held between them. "I was lending it to you."

He *was* cold, actually, until she sat on his lap. Now he had a different problem.

"You're gripping me rather hard, sir," she said tentatively. "I hesitate to mention it, but the fate of my trunk handle necessitates that I bring this to your attention."

He quickly set her back to the other seat.

"I didn't mean to wake you," she added.

But they were pulling into The George and Dragon at last, the wheels slowing. Thankfully! He needed a bed and time away from this strange, impertinent woman. And floor upon which to pace for a while, alone and unobserved, until his pulse was steadier, back to its usual rhythm. They'd travelled a fair distance that evening, and he felt as if he'd done most of it on foot.

She, on the other hand, seemed tireless. "Look how pretty the snow is," she said, looking through the window. "We shall be cozy here, shan't we, sir?"

He grunted, not at all certain.

The best that could be said for this inn, as far as J.P. recalled, was that he had found it clean of fleas in the past. As it was tonight, blanketed by glistening snow and surrounded by the warm amber of lanterns, it was a welcome, picturesque sight. Even J.P. could admit that much, as he looked at it through the eyes of an enthusiastic newcomer.

The innkeeper took them up a narrow staircase to small rooms— rustic but free of drafts. Having asked if there was anything else J.P. required, the landlord gave him a lit candle and a plate of bread and cheese, presumably meaning for the two of them to share, and left them to settle in until morning. Miss Follyot did not seem to mind that she was largely ignored, suggesting that this happened often. Fetching a candle from the box in her own chamber, she lit it from his.

"I bid you good evening, sir," she said brightly, her face shining in the light of that candle. "Sweet dreams, Mr. Thursday." She winked, turned and went into her room, bolting the door behind her.

Sweet dreams, indeed. He was not a boy. Even when he was one, his dreams had never been sweet.

Of course, the "Mr. Thursday" told him that she remembered something he wished she did not. A past encounter, she was bold enough to tease him about.

J.P. went to his own room, set his candle by the bed, tore off his gloves and warmed his bare fingers around that wavering, slender flame. The roof beams were low so he could not quite stand up straight and pacing was out of the question, so instead he sat on the bed to remove his boots and think about the strange woman in the room across the hall. The funny and fearless creature, who threw herself into life as if she had naught to lose.

He had never met anybody quite like her.

Why on earth would she get it into her head to tuck a blanket around him? It was her blanket, and she must have been cold too. Why think of him? She knew what he was. A cad. A Deverell.

If it was anybody else he truly would have suspected them of going through his pockets, but she was not like that. She was too honest, her face showing her every thought, unable to deceive, even when she tried to make up stories about an absentee fiancé.

His father always said that an honest face was a rarity in this world.

He felt a shiver and looked across the room at the window. It was fastened. Good.

But a shadow lurked there, another ghost from his past.

* * * *

Christmas 1867

Miss Bessie "Bluebell" Babcock was a songbird of the stage, an artiste of some notoriety among his university friends, so he had heard about her long before Jacob Dockery dragged him away from his studies to see her perform.

"Come on, old chap, put your books away. It's Christmas!"

From the stage she picked him out, tossing him a yellow flower from her costume, as she did at the end of her act every night. J.P. would have left it where it fell, but he was cheerfully advised by Jacob, a devotee of the lady's work, that this would be impolite and unchivalrous.

"Miss Bluebell has chosen you, old chap. She must have seen how sad you are and wants to elevate your spirits."

He was twenty. Other young men at university made the most of their time to do far more than study— in many cases to do anything *but* study— and some would envy him, as the target of Miss Bluebell's affections. Perhaps he should indulge, he'd thought. She was beautiful, like an oil painting, and he would like something pretty in his life, when he looked up from his books.

Thus he was swept along with her act for a while, became a part of it when she was off stage, but still performing. Not that he realized it at the time. He underestimated her talent as an actress and thought that the woman he knew in his bed was the real Bessie.

For the first few weeks of their relationship she managed to conceal the truth from him, always being bathed, powdered and perfumed when they were together, her lips smiling and eyes like blue glass. She put all of her energy into him when they were together. He had no idea what she did when they were not. Nor did he particularly care, or so he thought.

His father, on his way to London, called in to visit the university and was waiting in J.P.'s lodgings one evening when he walked in with Bessie. Naturally introductions must be made.

"The woman is cheap and tawdry," True Deverell said in his usual frank way, soon after she was gone. "But I suppose all men go through such a phase. Myself included."

True Deverell, even in advanced years, was handsome, a man who did not move down a street without being noticed and turning heads. J.P.'s mother said it was because he prowled rather than walked and it was natural human instinct to keep one's eye on a panther as it passed closely.

Bessie, of course, had fluttered her lashes and performed for the charming and notorious True Deverell, forgetting that his son was even in the room.

"I made my own share of mistakes as a young man, so perhaps I am a hypocrite to mention it. But I am thinking of your mother. She would be most disappointed in your choice, J.P." He'd put his head on one side. "Don't you think?"

Much to J.P.'s chagrin, it was a fact undeniable. He could picture his mother's face quite clearly if she ever met Bessie. Oh, she would be kind and gracious, but Bessie's extravagance and forward manner would make her wince. His father knew how reminding J.P. of his mother would have the deepest affect, naturally.

"She is using you for the money," his father had added casually. "I hope you mind your coin."

Which is when J.P. decided he knew more than his father in this matter. "She does not ask me to buy her anything," he protested.

"Not with words, I suppose. She's too clever and artful for that."

"I know what I do, sir."

"Then you're the first young man of twenty who does."

But J.P. would not be told otherwise by his father, who had suddenly decided to notice his youngest son.

John Paul. Very clever at his books. Takes after his mother. Nothing more to be said, except...*I thought I was done raising children.*

He did not know why the man bothered after all this time.

"Take care, John Paul. A man in the market for a house or a woman should always visit them at all hours of the day and night, before making a firm decision on the acquisition."

"I am sure my mother would love to be compared to the purchase of a house."

"Prepare yourself to be scandalized, boy, but your mother lived with me for two years before she agreed to marry me. What do you suppose she was doing all that time, but testing the floorboards and checking for woodworm in the rafters?"

His father's remarks about Bessie stayed with him. It was true; she did not ask him for money— not with words— but somehow he found himself buying her all manner of things.

The showy affection with which Bessie put her arms around him was another part of the stage act, he began to realize; like the face paint, frills and footlights, her time in his bed kept her looking and feeling youthful. She used him for that, as much as the money.

He generally only saw her in the evening, after her performance. So one day, he arrived earlier than expected at her dressing room and found her listless, crotchety and cursing at her maid, her face sallow without rouge and her hair matted. She could barely rise from the chaise, or open her eyes fully, until she had drunk three glasses of champagne. Finally her long-suffering maid carefully began to put her together, hoisting her into a bath and then a corset, while brushing the knots from her hair.

J.P. was shocked that his butterfly was actually a caterpillar. Even her voice was different— harsh and shrill.

He did not make the mistake of calling early upon her again, but he had the idea that he might help her live a life off stage, a truer one. He even bought her a new gown for Christmas, something more tasteful, so that he could take her to dinner and not have everybody pointing at them, whispering about "Miss Bluebell and that Deverell boy".

But she passed the gown on to her maid and said she was too tired to dine that night.

Her eyes had turned opaque as soon as she opened the package and saw the gown he'd bought her. Her smile became more fixed, less dazzling. Her light cooled.

He felt like a fool.

It occurred to him that she liked being stared at and whispered about; that she did not want a life off the stage; that she did not care to exist without footlights and the adoration of her audience, the lusty eyes of all men upon her. One man would never feed her vanity enough.

"The boy wants me to dress like a bleedin' nun," he heard her laugh to her maid as he stood outside her dressing room. "As if I ain't good enough for a Deverell."

Soon after that J.P. discovered that he was no longer her "favorite". She threw her yellow flowers to half a dozen other young men until she found another as wealthy and foolish.

Where was she now? Did Miss Bluebell still perform? He would not know; he never went to the theatre these days. Her time on the stage must surely have come to an end by now, ten years later. Or had she managed to keep going into her forties, extending her season in the lights, her maid winding her up carefully each day, buoying her laughter with champagne bubbles and polishing the tarnish from her shiny case?

He had tried with her— more so than with Mrs. Randall— but still he had not understood the woman. Perhaps he had no chance, since he would never see the real Bessie. Did a man ever see the real woman? Did he ever know her fully and completely and honestly?

Bessie, posed in her stage costume, stood in the corner of his room. Just briefly, like the flare of a match, he remembered how she once looked, up on the stage, smiling down at him. As fragile as glass, colorful only when light was cast upon it.

Now she cracked and shattered into tiny shards that fell and spun away across the floor.

In her place he saw his father standing there, hands behind his back, looking down at his boots. No... not at his boots, but at a little boy running in circles around his legs.

Was that J.P.? It must be.

And yet his father was smiling warmly down at him— in a way that J.P. did not remember— and then he crouched suddenly and lifted the little boy into his arms, only to keep him spinning in circles, high above his head, the two of them laughing, comrades in mischief. As he flew round and round his father's head, the boy saw sprigs of holly tucked around a framed painting on the wall, a pyramid of pears on the sideboard, a punch bowl with orange slices floating across its ruby surface.

"Put that boy down. You'll make him sick," said a woman.

"But he wants to fly," his father replied, "and as he's my son, it's my job to make certain he gets to do all that he wants."

"You'll spoil him and he'll be intolerable. Look what happened to us."

"Yes. He's my last chance, isn't he?" He lowered the boy to his broad shoulder. "I'd better make sure I do this one the right way and leave him to Olivia. Don't want to muck this one up too. She's a far better influence than I could ever be."

J.P. felt the heat emanating from his father, the slightly damp, grey-speckled hair against his cheek and the vibration of his deep laughter. He could smell the sea. His father must have just come in from his ride along the sands— an exercise he took daily, whatever the weather or season. Now he bounced his youngest son in his arms and laughed, his eyes crinkled up at the corners. "I'll have to spoil you when the others aren't looking," he whispered in the boy's ear.

How odd that he had never remembered that moment until now, and for those few breathless seconds it was so alive, vibrant with love and warmth.

The figures faded, and the little scene in the corner went dark again.

I may not be a little girl anymore, just as you are not a boy, but I wish my father were still alive so that I could visit him for Christmas. Miss Follyot's words rippled through his head, like warm bubbles at the sea's edge, creeping across the sand in whispers to wet his feet when he least expected it, when he thought he was safe and far enough away.

He blinked, rubbed his eyes and fell back onto the bed.

Really must try to sleep.

Beyond that wall, on the other side of his head, his traveling companion slept. If she slept at all. It was hard to imagine the steam engine of her mind stopped in a peaceful siding for long enough. Was the wall throbbing, or was that her still humming?

Oddly, it felt as if he knew her very well already, as if she had been there, in his life, for a long time.

Yet he had only just noticed her there.

She was a woman who did not hide. How could he not have seen her?

He scowled. Trying to tuck him in, for pity's sake. Telling him he had "lovely" eyes. Asking him questions! Winking!

Being so naive and soft-hearted she probably had sent her silk drawers to that man who advertized in the *Exchange and Mart*. She was the wide-eyed sort who fell prey to every unscrupulous villain out there.

But no, she was not stupid. She was simply very challenging to keep up with.

Something about her company was causing him to revisit the women and the Christmases of his past. Sorting through them, searching for something. Was it because she too was there, somewhere in that history, waiting to be found?

There was a vicarage tea party for the village children some sixteen or seventeen years ago. Perhaps you will remember little Anne?

He had the most disturbing notion that although he had forgotten her once before, she was about to make certain he would never do so again.

Or her trunk was, he mused, rubbing his knee.

* * * *

She heard a shout and sat up.

A thud. A sharp cry.

Anne put her coat over her nightgown and took her candle out into the narrow hall. "Mr. Deverell? Is everything—?"

His door opened. He was clutching a bolster from the bed, his face grey. "Damn mouse," he sputtered. "One of *your* friends, no doubt." As if she might have smuggled one with her on the journey.

"Just a mouse?" She walked into his room, and he backed away, still holding the bolster. "What did you mean to do with that? Smother the poor thing?"

"I certainly did not mean to make friends." He pointed. "It ran under the bed."

"Well, really, I daresay it came in out of the cold. Fancy a big man like you being afraid of a little mouse!"

"I am not afraid," he snapped. "It took me by surprise, that's all! I heard its little feet, scurrying..."

Anne knelt to look under the bed and found the mouse watching her with beady black eyes, whiskers twitching. "Pass me one of your boots. Or the chamber pot."

"But I don't want—"

"Sir, if you want me to help you, kindly do as I ask. It won't hurt your blessed boot."

Cursing under his breath, he slid one of his boots across the floor to her. After a short struggle she managed to capture the mouse and carried it to her own room across the hall, tragedy averted.

"He can stay in my room until the morning and then he won't bother you again," she said calmly. "I'll give him some of that bread and cheese, and a stern talking to in the meantime."

He finally lowered the bolster. "Thank you, Miss Follyot. Although it really was not necessary. I had everything under control. I am quite alright."

"Are you?"

He scowled.

"Don't look so panicked, I shall be the soul of discretion and never tell anybody. No charge for the rescue. It is all part of the adventure."

She thought it best not to point out that where there was one mouse there were surely many others.

* * * *

In the morning he woke to a bang and then the sound of laughter outside. He sat up, confused at first, until he remembered where he was and what had happened yesterday— who had happened— to stop his cogwheels.

He stumbled out of bed and limped to the window, knowing, somehow, that she was the one making the noise outside. The one who woke him from deep slumber.

The snow must have stopped falling soon after they arrived at the inn last night, for the scenery was still pretty and soft, the early sky tinted pink, like the inside of a conch shell, the trees still, bowed down under their fleecy coats. Occasionally clumps fell, freeing a branch that sprung upward in celebration.

Below his window, leaping about with an abundance of energy, was Miss Follyot, in her ugly brown bonnet and coat, but surely with her face frozen in the cold air. The vitality of youth had got her out of bed early, without aches and pains. Her cheeks were two bright roses against the white as she gathered another handful of snow, aimed, and threw it at his window.

He ducked, and it hit the window frame in any case.

But she laughed so hard that she fell backward into the snow. Which almost made him laugh too. He'd never seen a woman so careless about how she looked, so intent on pleasure that nothing else mattered.

Oops, probably should not let his mind wander into the realms of wild pleasure and how he might open her eyes to a great many new delights.

He hastily shut the window and moved out of her view. Would not want to encourage the woman in her foolish behavior, or let her artlessness lure his own mind into dangerous territory.

They ate breakfast below in the little dining room of the inn, and with renewed puffs of steam she resumed her chatter, asking him how he slept, whether he dreamed and what about, whether he thought it would snow again today or if it would melt. He answered her whenever he could fit a word in, but she did not seem to mind how brief his replies were. Would she notice if there were none?

Before he came down she had asked the innkeeper if he could provide a fresh cloth bandage for J.P.'s knee. "I hope it is better today," she said. "I thought about it last night and how clumsy it was of me to let my trunk fall into the street like that. Really I would not be surprised if you never spoke to me again."

"Miss Follyot, I told you to cleanse your mind of it. Please." He did not know how he felt about her taking the matter in hand. J.P. was accustomed to managing his own needs. "Surely you have frocks, shoes, or bonnets to be thinking about and fretting over. Is that not the usual fodder that fills a lady's mind? Or your wedding trousseau for the marriage to Mr. Claiborne Arbuthnot Darkwinters. The third, no less." He smirked.

"How could I not think of your kindness? Here you are, escorting me across the country at great cost and you were not planning a trip for yourself."

He picked up the innkeeper's bill, checking it over carefully as he always did. "I had no plans to travel, that is true, but I had no plans at all for Christmas." He sighed. "So you spoiled nothing. Does that make you feel better?"

She was entitled to that confession, he had decided, since she was honest about the trunk. And she had rescued him last night from the tiny, four-footed invader.

"Oh. No plans at all? Not even on a *Thursday*?"

He continued his study of the bill. "None. So no sympathy is required, Miss Follyot," he warned sternly.

The woman fell silent. Just like the night before, her mute pauses seemed ominous, more troubling

The Snow Angel

than her long speeches. It was, he supposed, like listening to a child at play in another room. When all was quiet one knew mischief was afoot.

"Why were you gallivanting about outside in the snow this morning? Surely that is not proper behavior for young ladies. Over the age of nine."

She shrugged. "How could I not go outside when I woke and saw the sheer beauty of it? That glistening down of snow, as yet unmarked, just waiting for my footsteps to leap upon it? Mother Nature would not make weather the way she does if she did not mean for us to appreciate it. Whatever our age."

"As a sane adult, I can appreciate it from indoors by glancing through a window, especially when it is bitter cold out."

"Then you are not fully enjoying Mother Nature's bounty."

"The weather, Miss Follyot, is a scientific occurrence involving the elements of temperature, moisture, air pressure and wind. It is not an event designed and manufactured by a mystical entity to please us."

"That is the most dull and uninspiring description of weather that I have ever heard."

"It is, nonetheless, the truth."

"Well, I like to be out in it," she asserted firmly, "however it is made."

"Then I am surprised you've managed to maintain that sterling health of which you boasted to me yesterday."

Her eyes sparkled as she looked across at him. "I suppose it is quite remarkable that I survived at all. One day, when I was a baby, my mother set me outside in a little, rocking wooden cot in the fresh air, because the house was steamy from the laundry. But while she was inside and busy, it rained, so suddenly and so hard, that a large puddle formed in our yard. In moments it became a sliding lake of mud and it swept me down into the river that crossed the foot of our garden. My mother came out and found me gone— thought I was lost forever. But they found me, a half hour later, floating merrily down the river in my wooden cot, as if it was Noah's Ark. Thus I was rescued. They said I was singing quite happily to myself, enjoying the ride. So, you see, I have never been afraid of the weather. I feel at home in it and know it will do me no harm."

"The rain swept you into the river?" Although he had found her to be an honest woman at heart, she clearly enjoyed occasional stories of a fantastical bent. It was an intriguing dichotomy of her character. Some women he'd met could lie freely in their daily life, but would think the telling of a story for entertainment childish and beneath them.

"I dreamed last night that we were buried under a snowdrift and had to dig our way out," she said, leaping to another subject, as was her habit. "That was your fault for putting the thought into my head yesterday. I do not suppose you had any interesting dreams, sir."

Since he had endured a very strange dream that seemed set in some far away future and included Miss Follyot, he was not about to tell her, so he said, "Nothing of interest to you, I fear."

"There you go again, sir, assuming you know what interests me."

"My dreams are private matters."

"But one can tell a great many things about a person from their dreams."

He assured her gravely, "Then you are obliged to make your analysis of me without them."

Which received from her a heartfelt sigh. "Seldom have I had less to work upon. You are a man of mystery, sir. Fortunately, I like mysteries and unwrapping parcels of many layers. I shall get to the bottom of your parcel before we have to say goodbye."

He stared at her, his heartbeat suffering a sudden jolt. "I hope you're not disappointed by what you find when you get there."

"Why should I be? The pleasure is in the journey as much as the destination."

"You are an optimist, madam."

"And you are determined never to laugh. I thought perhaps your teeth might be crooked and blackened with rot, but I see now in daylight that they are in very good condition, of sufficient number and in their proper places, so there is no excuse not to show them off."

"I am relieved you find my teeth acceptable."

"Are you never swept up in happiness and joy, Mr. Deverell? Not even at Christmas?"

"Not to excess, as far as I can recall."

"You never like to laugh?"

"One manages without it."

"But how much better your life would be, if you made time for a little merriment within it."

"Who says I have no merriment? One does not have to laugh out loud to be amused." And he liked teasing her, seeing the little puffs of frustration escape her soft lips in the cold air.

"I suppose you ration your excitement and the energy expelled upon it."

"Suppose away, madam. I would not want to spoil your own pleasure by curtailing your imagination."

She proceeded to mock his expression and he let her, his own mind drifting among the shadows of the past again.

* * * *

December, 1870

Mrs. Godfrey was his widowed landlady when he and Dockery first set up their shop together. She too was older than him and not hesitant in making her interest known. It was a cold winter, and she was well-padded.

Often, when he thought of their relationship in that long ago winter, that was how he remembered it most of all. They saved on the price of coal together.

She fed him very well, being an excellent cook, and she took good care of his clothes, mending them with a neat stitch, as needed, and tending stains with a diligence that suggested her life, and his, depended on it. She had even given him the occasional bath, shave and hair cut. Mrs. Edith Godfrey certainly took care of him.

They did not talk much of their lives, until one day he found her weeping over a little picture in an oval frame. She told him then of the child she lost when she was first married and how it had turned her husband against her, blaming her for a sickness that took the boy and was quite out of her hands. Her marriage was filled with quiet, unforgiving hate for the remainder of its years, until her husband died.

"My boy would have been about your age now," she said, her eyes wet and red. "I always think of him at Christmas."

Damnable Christmas. It had a lot to answer for.

Nothing J.P. could say to her would stem the tears and he was left at her side, feeling awkward, trying stupidly to comfort. And all the time shocked that she was old enough to be his mother. He had known she was older, but not *that* much older.

After that he began to realize that he was her substitute son. The hair brushing, the feeding until his waist thickened, the management of his clothing...it was motherly. Now it felt "smotherly" and disturbing.

He moved into the offices above the shop at the first opportunity and was left even more confused by women after that. Not only was he utterly unaware of what they were thinking, or what they wanted from him; now he was equally nonplussed about what they saw in him.

Women seemed to communicate in a different language. As for Christmas, it was rapidly becoming his least favorite time of year as the discomforting memories and unpleasant revelations steadily amassed.

He was like a man with his history— or his Christmases— passing before his eyes, before his life came to a sudden end. Again, Miss Follyot was the cause of it. Must be. She would be the death of him, it seemed.

But when she took charge of his new bandage and tried tucking him in with her blanket, it did not feel the same as when Mrs. Godfrey made a fuss of him. It did not feel intrusive. She expected nothing in return and there was no sadness in the gesture, just concern for his well being. Extraordinary.

"*We never know how long we've got,*" Jacob Dockery whispered again in his ear. "*You must make the most of your time. Don't sit here alone. You've things to do. Life to live, love to give.*"

Love. It happened occasionally to other people, but not for J.P. He did not believe in it for himself, any more than he believed in the spirit of Christmas. That too, happened to other people.

* * * *

Once the carriage and horses were ready, her trunk refastened and the bill paid, they made their way out into the snow, ready to continue their journey.

Then, suddenly, Miss Follyot made a garbled excuse about forgetting something and dashed back inside. He waited for her, holding the door impatiently, and finally she came running out again. She smiled her thanks, before stepping up into the carriage, looking flushed and pleased with herself.

He decided not to ask about it. No doubt she would tell him soon enough, since she was incapable of keeping anything to herself for long.

Chapter Ten

She stared out at the passing scenery and wildlife along the snow-clad hedgerows. One hand she kept in her coat pocket, her fingers carefully holding something out of his sight.

Really she did not know why she kept it secret for now, but it felt the thing to do. He would only roll his eyes and huff, no doubt. Like her brother, he must think her addled too by now and would take nothing she said seriously.

If she told him of her snow angel, would it just be more chatter to which he barely paid heed? Perhaps she should be discreet. She could not imagine that he would smile and say he remembered.

He did not even believe her Noah's Ark story and generally people did, because she told it so well, complete with actions and gestures.

But not him. He was skeptical of everything she said, looked at her as if she might be trying to trick him in some way just by her mere presence in his company. As if she might not truly exist.

In actual fact, it was her brother who put her cot in the river when she was a babe, hoping she'd be washed away and he could go back to being an only child. But it was raining, so her version of events was not such a great stretch. And a much better story than the tale of a jealous sibling.

Sometimes real life needed a little embellishment. See, she knew that, even in her cot.

Last night she had lain awake for some time, making the story of her journey into a tale of extraordinary survival against the odds, preparing to enthrall the other ladies of Mrs. Smith's boarding house when she returned to London. For an hour at least, before the incident of the mouse, she had listened to the sounds of the Deverell in the next room, moving about restlessly, occasionally banging his head on a low beam and cursing colorfully.

He had told her that he knew the place, had stayed there before, and it was clear the innkeeper remembered him.

Had he stayed there with other women? There must have been women in his life— like Mrs. Marvington. Anne was not that naive, whatever her landlady assumed. Her brother's behavior, both before his marriage and after, had opened her eyes to all that when she was still young. A burden of her place as lady of the house at such a young age.

"You realize you'll have to marry the girl now," she remembered hearing her father shout at Wilfred one day, as she and her little sister stood in the kitchen making mince pies, pretending not to eavesdrop.

"I suppose I shall," her brother replied, sullen.

"And you will take that post at the bank."

Wilfred's groan echoed through the wall from her father's study.

"I cannot afford to pay off all your debts," her father had snapped, sounding angrier than she had ever heard him. "Not if the girls are to have any dowry at all."

"Father, nobody worries about dowries anymore. That is old fashioned. Besides, only Lizzie is likely to marry, for she has an easy temper and a fair enough face. But Anne will always live here with you. She does not have Lizzie's placid, gentle manner. She's not going anywhere."

Anne's heart fell to her toes, and Lizzie spun around to look at her. But she put a finger to her lips in warning. The men must have forgotten they were still in the kitchen and had not gone out yet to the market.

On the other side of the wall, her brother scoffed loudly. "When Lizzie marries she can keep Anne as a housekeeper or a nanny. What else can possibly be done with her? What portion would she need? It's *Anne* for pity's sake. Anne who talks to the angels and insists she prefers toads to princes."

"Well...enough about that now... this is about you, Wilfred. Let us return to that. You will have a wife and soon a child too. They will be your responsibility. Time to put your wastrel habits aside and become an adult who earns his own keep. Your mother's uncle has been kind enough to offer you a clerk's post at the bank in Aylesbury, and it is the best we can do now."

A bank clerk's post came with a good salary and holidays, and was given only to those of exceptional character— a position much sought after. By anybody but Wilfred Follyot.

Her brother, of course, had far more fanciful ideas for himself than working in a dull bank, but his own missteps had led him to this. It was one problem he could not get out of or blame upon anybody else, although no doubt he tried.

"Poor Wilf," Lizzie had whispered, drooping with pity for the ingrate Wilfred, even her braids falling limp.

"He's going to marry and work in a bank," Anne had replied. "He's not having a limb amputated."

"But he does not sound very happy at the prospect. He must not be in love with her, whoever she is."

"Well, he should have thought of that before he got her into trouble." At seventeen she understood a great deal more about such matters than her twelve-year-old sister, naturally. Anne knew then that she would never allow herself to be cornered into marriage. She would never settle just to save herself from spinsterhood.

"What do you mean? What sort of trouble?"

The study door banged shut, the men's voices reduced to a low, angry hum.

Her brother's transgression and their father's anger put a dampener on Christmas that year. Anne remembered fearing that from then on all Christmases would be difficult and not as joyful as they had once been. That nothing would be the same ever again. They were growing up and facing grown up problems.

That was almost five years ago, and Wilfred was now the father of three. He was also plump as a stuffed goose, red-faced and gouty. He looked twice his age. Bad habits told on a man eventually, even if he was born with good looks. Such a waste.

In Mr. Deverell's case it did not seem to be bad habits, but a hundred years of worry that weighed him down. He took life far too seriously, whereas her brother never had. She was surprised to find a Deverell so well behaved. He did not drink to excess and had not tried to seduce her. He had screamed at a mouse and blushed at the mention of silk drawers. At least, she thought he had blushed about that. Something had made him hot.

Today her companion read his paper in daylight, while she slyly took her chance to study him more thoroughly— his brows and eyelashes, at least, since they were visible above the newspaper. Mr. Deverell's looks improved upon acquaintance, she decided, although she could see how he might frighten people on first impression. But thunderstorms, bulls and guard dogs of all sizes had never scared Anne.

And now she knew something special about this beast. Something interesting and unexpected. Well, two things actually. He was afraid of mice. And he had very clever hands.

She carefully felt the object in her pocket— the paper bill she had retrieved from their breakfast table at the last minute— and wondered again if she should mention it to him. However, if he dismissed it as foolish notion, as a nothing, she couldn't bear it.

Could it be a coincidence that he would brush aside, disposing of the idea, as was the fate suffered by so many of Anne's imaginings?

Perhaps she would keep it her secret and enjoy it thus without him bringing her flights of fancy back down to dreary earth. He would not appreciate it as she did, in any case.

Her gaze returned to the carriage window. For once— *for once*— she would hold her tongue and keep something she knew to herself.

How much better it would be if he remembered, without her prompting. She thought her heart might burst.

The horses pulled them easily along now. Last night, as she lay in bed, restless, she had hoped they might be snowed in, unable to leave the inn for just a little longer, but alas it was not to be. Unless it snowed again. She peered up at the sky hopefully. Just one extra day of adventure would be enough, surely. But she would not want the horses to suffer, or poor Jarvis, the coachman, who seemed an amiable fellow, dragged along on this trip because of Anne.

She sighed and shook her head. "Does Mr. Jarvis have family that he will miss for Christmas, sir?"

"Jarvis is extremely well paid and has no wife. Spare your pity for him too. He is probably better off than a great many young men."

"But still—"

"When we get to Roscarrock he will be well rewarded. My father keeps a very good cook at home, who has a remarkably pretty niece."

"You did not tell me that yesterday when we set off. Instead you let me think I was putting everybody out."

He said nothing, but she caught sight of a slight smirk as they went over a rut and he lowered his paper briefly before turning a page.

"At least I know there is something that entertains you then," she muttered.

In a flash his eyes lifted to hers. "Yes. You do."

* * * *

She imagined he was a prince, noble and serious, rescuing her in his carriage, having kissed her awake. Well, not kissed. Slapped, perhaps. Wilfred maintained that was a more efficient way to wake somebody.

"My dear Miss Follyot, you must come with me to my kingdom in the sea," said her imaginary royal, laying aside his newspaper, his sleeves gleaming with jewels as he put out his hand to her, palm up. "I shall take you away from all this, and you will never again work at Lockreedy and Velder. Put all that behind you."

"But I like it there," she heard herself utter softly and apologetically.

They went over a bump that knocked his glittering crown slightly askew. "A princess cannot work in a shop. You will be safer with me."

"Stifled, you mean."

The prince looked askance as he took his hand back and adjusted his crown. "I'm supposed to rescue you. That's primarily what princes do."

"But I do not need rescuing. I need—"

Suddenly the prince transformed into a fierce-eyed warlord, his cheeks marked with mud, scars and speckles of blood, his hair hanging long, loose and matted to his armor-clad shoulders. He grabbed her by the waist and dragged her over his lap.

"Be silent, captive slave. Now you are my prize!"

Enveloped in the folds of his fur-lined cape and the thick odor of sweat, she struggled against his hard embrace. "I suggest you let me go, sir. You'll find other women more subservient and docile. I'll be far too incommodious, as you said before." *Bang*, went her elbow into his dented metal chest.

"We'll stop here for fresh horses and to eat. As good a place as any."

She was back to reality.

Ah, not a prince or a medieval knight, just a Deverell. She was actually quite glad about it. There was much to be said for a man who smelt pleasant and was not all groping hands.

He had been looking out of the window, and now he turned his gaze to her.

"Miss Follyot, you breathe heavily. I do hope you are not ill. Perhaps you caught cold yesterday."

She could swoon, she thought, closing her eyes briefly. He might sweep her up in his arms and rush her into the tavern, shouting for a doctor as her arm hung limply in the cold air. He would sit by her bed until she recovered, despite the fact that it was improper. Nobody would likely dare tell J.P. Deverell what to do.

But no, she was in the rudest of health. There was nothing to be done about that. Her brother had tried often enough.

So she smiled, resigned to the tragedy of her unromantic good health. "I am rather hungry, sir."

"Yes," he muttered, looking puzzled suddenly. "So am I."

Good lord! Information volunteered about his inner workings, without her having to pry for it.

* * * *

The day passed swiftly. Mr. Deverell seemed very interested now in her employment at Lockreedy and Velder's Universal Emporium, asking about her fellow workers and what they thought of the place too.

"When I received my aunt's letter and had to ask Mr. Shepherd, the head clerk, for some days off, I thought he would have no alternative but to refuse. After all, this is a busy time of year and he would have to explain my absence to Mr. Lockreedy. But he was most kind and understanding. He works hard every day and is always cheerful, despite the fact that Mr. Lockreedy is difficult to please."

"Difficult to please?"

She nodded solemnly. "I asked him once why Mr. Lockreedy never comes down to the shop floor, and Mr. Shepherd said we should be glad of it, for we would only be shouted at. He said Mr. Lockreedy demands perfection from everybody and has a fierce temper, so we girls should stay out of his way. I wanted to thank Mr. Lockreedy personally for hiring me, you see, when I first started, but Mr. Shepherd said it would be the last anybody would see of me if I did."

"Did he indeed?"

"Mr. Lockreedy does not know how to accept gratitude, he said, and prefers to do his good deeds in anonymity. I think it's rather tragic that the poor old man shuts himself away from life in that office at the top of the stairs."

"Well, he has your landlady to keep him company at night occasionally. According to the ladies of that boarding house."

"True. I often wonder whether he watches us through a peephole, or whether he simply trusts Mr. Shepherd to tell him everything that happens. Poor Mr. Shepherd. He's run off his feet every day and then he must report to the ogre in his lair each evening before he goes home."

"I daresay Mr. Shepherd is very well compensated."

"Mr. Lockreedy has languished in a considerable state of melancholy since his partner, Mr. Velder, passed away. They were devoted old friends, despite the fact that they were very different men, so Mr.

Shepherd says. Mr. Velder used to worry about his friend because he enjoyed little life outside the business."

He said nothing, and she supposed he was tired of that subject.

"In my opinion the hampers we sell at Lockreedy and Velder are every bit as fine as those from Fortnum and Mason. Better, in fact, because they are well stuffed to the corners with provisions and not filled with more straw than is necessary. I mean to say, it is all very exciting to fumble through straw and discover treats hidden there, but it's a disappointment of some magnitude when the retrieval of those surprises is over in very little time, leaving one's hands full of more straw than treat." She paused. "I'm shocked you are not acquainted with us, Mr. Deverell. We are the very finest store in London, and new branches are soon to be opened elsewhere in the country."

"With such a glowing endorsement, I can see I shall have to amend the oversight when I return to London."

Oh, would he come to see her there, she wondered. A quick twinge of excitement twisted through her stomach at the thought. The other girls would be all agog.

We must stop meeting this way, Mr. Deverell. People will talk.

"And tell all your friends too," she said. "Assuming you have some."

He looked at her in a faintly amused manner. Although she supposed it could be wind or indigestion. "Surprisingly, I do. More than your unfortunate Mr. Lockreedy, in any case."

Anne had just speared another potato on her fork when, looking through the tavern window behind his head, she spied a familiar figure alighting from a barouche box in the yard outside. The young woman stepped very cautiously over the ice and snow, her hand and elbow gripped by the attentive gentleman in her company.

No. Oh, no. Please.

Lizzie. In that startled moment between mouthfuls, it seemed unthinkable to Anne that anybody else should be out on that road in this weather; what right did they have? It was inconceivable that they had any reason to travel.

But alas, that was Mr. and Mrs. George Ingram— Anne recognized her brother-in-law's ginger whiskers above the collar of his coat, as he made his slow, halting trip across the yard with her sister held beside him like a fragile, china ornament, her toes barely allowed to touch the ground.

Anne's heartbeat had dropped to the same unsteady pace as their tentative steps. She glanced at the door. In a minute or so they would walk in and undoubtedly her sister would soon see her there, for the room was not large.

"If you are in agreement, Miss Follyot, I shall ask if they have rooms free for the evening," said her escort.

Wait. *What?* It was only afternoon and he wanted to stay?

"This is a pleasant area," he added, eyes darting guiltily from side to side before he fixed his gaze on the salt cellar. "There is a lake not far from here with some very charming views. I thought we might take a moment from our journey and enjoy—"

"No," she exclaimed, setting down her fork. "We should travel on to the next place. I do not think the rooms here would be as comfortable."

He squinted at her, one hand poised in the motion of taking out his fob watch. "Is there something amiss?"

"I would rather get farther along on our journey tonight, sir. We are making good time, you said yourself that at this rate, and barring more snowfall, we can be in Cornwall by late tomorrow. Why stop now?" He had not yet remembered the Snow angel. They needed more time together, and Lizzie was about to put a stop to it all by waking her from this very pleasant dream.

"I see," he muttered, looking down at the bill. "Yes, we do not want to drag it out longer than necessary, do we?"

He had misunderstood, but she could not mention her sister's presence. If she did he would think it very odd that Anne did not want to stay and greet her. He would think it even odder if he learned that her sister had planned to collect Anne from the boarding house on Thursday evening, but that she had chosen another route instead— the one suggested by her aunt, who was innocent of any other alternative on offer.

Lizzie wanted to surprise their aunt in Widecombe, apparently, and so had said nothing to anybody except Anne about making the journey. In the meantime, Anne had received her letter from Aunt Follyot and quickly decided a Deverell was preferable company to her newly married sister.

If Lizzie saw her there now, she would want Anne to continue on with them in that fancy carriage. The Ingrams would insist.

It was typical of Lizzie to think that a surprise at Christmas was a good idea, despite their aunt's small house and even smaller budget, but her little sister seldom thought her actions through fully, or weighed the inconvenience to others— the consequence of being the youngest in the family, cosseted by everybody and having no responsibility. Lizzie had never even been obliged to fasten her own boot buttons, for Anne was always there to do it for her from the time when her fingers were too small to grasp the hook. No doubt Mr. Ingram did it for her now, unless he'd employed a maid to look after his wife, which was more than likely considering the manner in which he fluttered and cooed around her.

Anne hastily sorted through her choices.

She could say that she had never received Lizzie's letter, of course. She could say that Mr. Deverell had been dragged away from his business in London, solely to escort her across the country, and that therefore she must stay with him in his carriage; it would be the height of rudeness to turn her back on his graciousness. But it was likely he would eagerly accept the chance to be rid of her and go on alone— either forward, or back to London. And Lizzie had a tendency to whine, which would embarrass everybody. Anne strongly suspected that Mr. Deverell had no tolerance for whining and would give his passenger up immediately rather than listen to her sister complain and wheedle.

It was decided therefore. If Lizzie saw her tonight, her adventure with Mr. Deverell would be too soon ended, and just when she was making inroads through his frown.

She quickly buttoned her coat— something her own fingers had always managed, even when they were very small and plump as grubs in a compost pile. "Let us make all good speed then."

"You have not finished your supper."

She laughed lightly. "A lady should always leave something on her plate."

Through wary eyes he watched her fingers as they thrust another button through its hole. "Do you know those people, by chance?" he inquired.

"What people?"

"The couple who just came in."

"I cannot say they are familiar to me. I'll wait for you in the carriage. Shall I fetch Mr. Jarvis?"

With that she ducked out through the kitchen to find the coachman and alert him to the necessity of their hasty departure.

Chapter Eleven

He knew he should not have listened to her at the last stop. Now, it was midnight and they were stranded at the next coaching inn on the road— a crowded, noisy, smelly place with only one, small room left vacant in the attic.

"I'll sleep with Jarvis in the stables," he said, trying to keep the edge out of his voice. "You must have the room, of course, Miss Follyot."

"Oh, but I feel terrible. This is all my fault."

Through gritted teeth, he managed a tight, "Never mind. What is good enough for the horses, I'm sure, is good enough for us. The straw will keep us from freezing."

She squeezed her hands together, her face scarlet. "I am wretched. No, I cannot take the room. I would never sleep for worrying."

"Well, somebody must take it, and the three of us cannot sleep in one room together, can we? I know you wanted adventure, madam, but your aunt entrusted your welfare to me. I'm certain she would shoot me where I stand if she knew I allowed you to contemplate such an idea. I may be a Deverell, but that is beyond even me."

"There is no cause to protest quite so much. We could have kept our clothes on."

"Even you cannot be that naive, Anne Follyot. This is not one of your novels."

"Are you suggesting the temptation would be beyond me? Have you forgotten Mr. Darkwaters?"

"How could I forget the infamous explorer who prevents you from trying to seduce me? I am ever in his debt."

Suddenly a hand reached through the crowd and tapped his coat sleeve with long, graceful fingers. "J.P. Deverell! Good god! What are you doing here?"

Jostled by the crowd he turned awkwardly, trying to erase his scowl at the same time. "Lady Greville." Unfortunately, the mob was too closely packed in for him to get away before she advanced closer.

"What are you doing here?" she repeated loudly above the ruckus.

"I am on my way to Cornwall."

Her eyes gleamed, the lashes elegantly lowered and raised again as she took him in from head to toe. Somehow she moved closer, her feet finding their way through the surge of thrusting people. "Going home? How long has it been?"

"I... couldn't say."

"It must be four years at least, since you took this road. Since the last time I saw you. I believe you've grown. Another few inches at least." She chuckled drowsily, her gaze skimming upward again. Slowly and pointedly.

He became aware of his young companion watching this exchange with wide eyes. Aware of her curious nature and wayward mind, he decided to get it over with quickly and nip whatever story she was concocting soundly in the bud.

Bloody ghosts of Christmas past! When would he be done with them? Did he really need to be beaten over the head with it? Yes, yes, so he'd made a few misjudgments when it came to women. They could stop haunting him now; he was sorry. He was damnably sorry he'd never paid more attention to the woman in the ugly brown bonnet and the moth-holed ribbon.

On a soft sigh, he muttered, "May I introduce Miss Anne Follyot. A family friend. I am taking her to see her aunt." He looked down at her. "Miss Follyot, this is Lady Greville. An acquaintance."

The girl gave a curtsey of sorts. Probably the best she could manage in that crowd. "Your ladyship. I am delighted to meet you."

"Mutual, I'm sure." But Lady Greville had quickly looked over his companion and evidently saw nothing interesting. She turned her shoulder to Anne, slid her hand under J.P.'s arm and beamed up at him, showing all her teeth. "You won't find a room free and the food here is terrible. Here's an idea! Why not come home with me? It's only a mile off the road. But you know that. You know I have plenty of room and what a wonderful, generous hostess I am."

Yes, he knew. He had no intention of going there, but before he could say anything, Miss Follyot chirped up from his other side. "Oh, that would be splendid, your ladyship. How kind of you to offer, for we were just wondering what might be done, were we not, Mr. Deverell?"

He cleared his throat. "But I think—"

"That's settled then," Lady Greville purred, patting his arm with her other hand. "You and your...little friend...must come to Wicklowe House at once. We shall have a glass of mulled wine in front of the fire and by the time the horses are settled in the stable, the beds will be warm, aired and awaiting your tired heads."

There was nothing else to be done. They needed rooms and she offered plenty to choose from, all warm and dry and free of fleas. He would simply have to put up with any other difficulties in order to give Miss Follyot and Jarvis a comfortable evening.

Besides, he could keep Lady Greville at bay for a few hours. There was a time when he'd found such a task impossible, but he was older now and wiser.

Surely she was too.

* * * *

Wicklowe House, Near Bournemouth, Dorset, Christmas 1873

House parties were not generally part of J.P.'s calendar. He preferred small gatherings with people he knew well, but, as usual, this was something to which Jacob Dockery dragged him along.

"I am in love," he'd said, smiling. "And I want you to meet her."

"What on earth for?" After all, Jacob had been "in love" many times before.

"I know what you're thinking, old chap. This time, it's different. You'll see. She is the loveliest of creatures, so amiable and sweet-natured. In fact, you might fall in love with her too. Hmm." A finger to his lips. "Perhaps you had better not come."

J.P. had given him a look. "I believe you know me well enough after fourteen years of this acquaintance to know the likelihood of me falling into anything as asinine and reckless as love." But he was curious and anxious for his friend. He'd seen Jacob make a fool of himself over women too many times. He decided he had better go and see this miraculous woman for himself.

Isabel Carlyle turned out to be a small, quiet, earnest young woman. Nothing at all that J.P. had expected. He was pleasantly surprised. In Isabel's company, Jacob seemed settled and content as he had never been before. His eyes no longer roved the room for something more interesting. He devoted his attention to Isabel and made her smile, bringing her out of her timid shell every time he came near. In each other's company they shone.

"It is all quite sickeningly sweet, is it not?" Lady Greville, their hostess, had whispered in J.P.'s ear.

He was, in fact, feeling quite envious of his friend at that moment. If only he could find a woman that would look at him that way. Alas, it did not seem to be possible.

"Poor little Miss Carlyle has led a sheltered, dreary life under her father's thumb," she added. "We must take care not to frighten her. I daresay Sir Alistair Carlyle thinks this house is Sodom and Gomorrah. If he knew his precious daughter had crossed my threshold, he would explode in outrage."

But Isabel was staying that winter with a cousin, who apparently kept fewer rules than her strict, protective father, and that was where Jacob had met her.

"Your friend, Dockery, insisted I invite her to Wicklowe House," said Lady Greville, with a husky chuckle. "I warned him that if her father gets wind of it, I shall blame him entirely for corrupting her and proclaim my innocence in the whole affair."

Rather than spend the next few days observing his best friend's descent into gooey-eyed oblivion, J.P. had quickly looked for something else to occupy his time. That was when he realized he had become the target of Lady Greville's admiration. She was a restless, somewhat scandalous widow with a passion for life and an undisguised lust for young men. Rumor had it that she had "done away" with the baron, her husband, by feeding him soup with chopped tiger's whiskers sprinkled into it. (*Hmm, a story perhaps Miss Follyot would enjoy*). In any case, she was left the house and contents in his will, and since the baron's daughters by a previous marriage were all grown up and gone away in disgust, she liked to fill the house with other young people. The wilder and more notorious the better. It was her way, he supposed, of getting vengeance on the society that snubbed her.

Lady Greville very much enjoyed her widowed freedom and J.P. enjoyed it too, for a few days before Christmas four years ago. Then, on his way back after visiting his family, he stayed with her again. She wanted him to remain longer, but he felt himself in danger of being trapped there, like a fly in a spider's web. Too much luxury and decadence could go to a man's head, and he had work to do. There was only so long he could lay abed.

"Surely you do not need to work," she had mewled in complaint, rolling over in the sheets as he left her bed. "You're a Deverell."

People liked to say his father was the richest self-made man in England. Although how anybody could know that for sure, J.P. had no idea. His father's fortune was like an iceberg, only a little of it visible above the ocean's surface. True Deverell treasured his secrets and kept plenty locked away, items he'd purchased anonymously at auctions around the world to add to his private collection. He enjoyed knowing he'd outfoxed those who looked down upon his humble beginnings as a foundling. In that way he was rather like Lady Greville— both outsiders, the main difference being that while his father did not care to be accepted by society, Lady Greville secretly burned inside to become a part of it.

"Despite my father's wealth," he had replied to her complaint, "he encourages his offspring to find purpose for themselves out in the world and make their own mark, not to rely on inherited bounty."

"*An education,*" his father would say, "*is the most precious thing I can provide for you. Then you must make of it what you will.*" Never having enjoyed the advantage of a fine, formal education himself, True wanted his boys to have everything he never had.

Over the years, when they were in trouble of one sort or another, he used his wealth to help them out, but as he reminded them all, "*The more you cost me now, the less your share when I'm gone.*" He had finally learned that throwing money at a problem did not help it go away for long.

But J.P. never asked his father for anything, never caused any trouble. Nothing that his father was obliged to know about. He thought of himself as self-sufficient.

"I like to work," he'd told Lady Greville. "It keeps my feet on the ground."

"You *like* to work? You choose *that* over me!"

"Yes," he'd answered frankly, his mind already on the journey ahead.

Apparently, she did not like that honesty; her vanity was insulted, when he thought she would be grateful to him for not beating about the bushes. Again he had misunderstood a woman. He thought she had surely been around long enough to know what was good for her and what was not. And since this was a coupling that satisfied only shallow, temporary, physical needs, extending it indefinitely could not be any better for her than for him.

But she did not see that. Or did not want to.

What did women need from him? Was the truth worse than a lie in their minds, when it did not suit their plans?

So they did not part on good terms. She unsheathed her claws when he simply got dressed and left without even participating in the argument she wanted. But days later, her temper cooled, she wrote him a letter, pouting and contrite, inviting him back to Wicklowe House whenever he came that way.

Another reason to avoid taking this road home.

When he did not respond to her letters, she tried to get to him through Jacob, meanly whispering into Isabel Carlyle's ears in an effort to turn her against the young man. J.P. discovered what she was up to and stepped in to put a stop to it.

"I merely tell the Carlyle girl what she needs to hear," Lady Greville protested, after he had agreed to meet her at a hotel in London. "She ought to be warned against gentlemen like you and your friend, or she will be used and tossed aside, as I have been."

"I did not set out to *use* you, Maria," he replied quietly. "I did not toss you aside. I thought we were of the same mind and need. You are no innocent and could not have expected a lasting affair or an engagement. I gave you no expectation of the sort."

"When you came to my bed, your attentions led me to believe we would have an exclusive, committed, long-lasting relationship. Why should I not think that and hope for it? I am not the sort of woman who takes young men randomly to her bosom."

Well, he decided to ignore the last, sizeable fib— he knew of at least three men— and addressed the other remarks. "You had an exclusive, committed relationship with your husband, Baron Greville, but it does not seem to have pleased you as much as your widowhood, which has left you free to dine with any man you choose. Why would you want to bind yourself again to one man?"

"My husband was an old man, whose touch repulsed me. Of course my marriage was not happy. Not for me."

"Yet you did marry him. Nobody forced you, did they?"

"It was a marriage of convenience. I needed a home and money. I did what I had to do."

"Perhaps, Madam, since you admit that *you* use men for your own convenience, you should not be surprised when you feel as if the same has been done to you."

She had thrown things at him, cursed the air that he breathed, and then went directly to Isabel Carlyle's father to tell him of his daughter's unguarded passion for the "unsuitable" and "shameless" Jacob Dockery. Unbeknownst to Jacob, J.P. again intervened on his behalf, this time visiting Isabel to assure her of his dearest friend's love for her. He did not waste his time going to the father. Such men could not be reasoned with. But he appealed to Miss Carlyle and asked her, with sincerity and his usual blunt honesty, to please not give up on his friend who would be intolerable to live and work with, unless he persuaded her to marry.

To Jacob, naturally, he acted as if the very idea of marriage appalled him. He never wanted his friend to know what he'd done to ensure that it was brought about. He did not like it when people felt obliged to repay favors.

"Is she perhaps not in full possession of her wits?" he muttered, when Jacob informed him of their plans to marry. It was only what his friend expected him to say, of course. It would have been odd and wrong if he said anything like congratulations. Jacob might even have considered it bad luck.

J.P. did not forget the wrath of Lady Greville, the savagery of which her mean temper was capable, and he very much doubted she'd forgiven him.

Now, thanks to Anne Follyot, he was once again forced into her company.

If his traveling companion had not insisted they drive on earlier and had agreed to stay at the last coaching inn instead, they would not have encountered Lady Greville tonight. But no, Miss Follyot was adamant that they travel as many miles as possible that day. His company must be boring her and no doubt she was desirous to get to her aunt.

Had he not been courteous today and taken an interest in her stories? He had even thought of delaying their journey a while for some sight-seeing that might please her. Again, he thought crossly, what the devil did women want?

But when Anne Follyot looked at him, he felt as if he was the only man in her life. He did not know what to do about it. What to do with this woman.

All he knew was that he liked the way she looked at him and he wanted to impress her. He did not want her disappointed at all, when she finally unwrapped his "parcel".

He was utterly knocked off course. Another first for J.P.

* * * *

Lady Greville's house was very grand. Anne, who had never been a guest inside such a house, felt herself to shrink about half the size as soon as she entered the echoing hall in her scuffed, thick boots. It was the sort of house in which only delicate slippers were ever worn by women of greater elegance and sophistication than herself.

An extravagant number of candles were already lit, even before the mistress of the house entered. Clearly there was no budget here, no counting out and careful distribution of candles, but waste on a scale that would cause Mrs. Smith apoplexy. Held in large, gold-painted, heavy candelabra and placed on tables against the walls, their bright glow revealed intriguing vignettes that only hinted at the size of the space and the height of that ceiling. It felt cavernous. Here and there she caught a gleam of gilt on delicate little chairs and console tables. The light flickered and caressed the marble curves of elegant statues, and danced across smug faces in portraits that were larger than life, their frames festooned with golden scrolls, puffing cherubs and bunches of grapes. Wherever she walked she was afraid of leaving a mark, or breaking some priceless antique, so she stood very still with her arms at her sides.

"You will find the beds here far more comfortable than the inn," said their hostess as she glided, graceful as a pink swan, across the fine carpet, having been relieved of her coat and hat by a liveried, rather annoyed-looking footman. "Take Miss Foster's coat and hat too, William," she snapped.

Although embarrassed to expose her old frock for the lady's critical gaze, Anne had no choice. The footman now glowered at her with his hand out, and she would not like to make him more irritated than he was already. For a girl who never had anybody take her hat and coat before, it was an experience. Where was he going to take it? How would she get it back?

From his expression she was only surprised he did not drop it directly on the floor.

"The name is Miss Follyot," said a low voice— Mr. Deverell's, she realized, as he came to stand beside her. Who else could it have been? But the size of the hall and the height of the ceilings made everything sound different, and the portraits seemed to be staring down at her with moving eyes. She was certain they were outraged by the sorry sight of her. Their mouths were pinched, ready to "Boo" her existence.

"Of course," said Lady Greville, both brows lifted in slender arches. "Miss Follyot. Do excuse me." Her face loomed closer. How quickly her lips moved from shouting at the footman to smiling. "Won't you come into the drawing room? William! Bring wine for my guests."

"It is a very beautiful house, your ladyship," said Anne, putting one booted foot carefully before the other, as if she walked a tightrope.

"You have no other guests at present, Lady Greville?" said Mr. Deverell, sounding almost relieved, but not quite.

"No. You find me all alone and at your disposal. I had just seen Lady Armstrong away on the mail coach this evening. She has been with me this past month, and I must say she was dreary company." She laughed. "I am glad to be rid of her. So very tiresome! While she was here, nobody else wanted to come, I suppose because they knew how dour she would be. My entertainment, as you can imagine, has been exceedingly scarce."

"Is Lady Armstrong not a friend of yours and recently bereaved?" asked Mr. Deverell.

"Of course." She placed a hand to her forehead and laughed again. "That would explain her grim wardrobe and sour face! I quite forgot. I do hate it when people go on grieving when one can no longer summon the sympathy. I mean, there is a limit to patience. For how long am I supposed to give up my entertainment when the dead person is nothing to me? I really do wish grieving people would not go out into society, just because the official mourning period is ended. If they are not ready to be amusing, they should stay at home and mop their tears in private."

Anne stared, but before she might be tempted to make comment, Mr. Deverell swung around to face her, his heels together, hands behind his back, head slightly inclined, a very meaningful look upon his face. Eventually she realized he meant for her to sit. When she did, he sat beside her on the couch, despite the fact that Lady Greville had gestured for him to sit by her chair instead.

His closeness immediately changed the air in the room for Anne. She had spent more than thirty hours in his company, but they had sat across from each other, in the carriage and in taverns along the way.

Apart from the occasion of the blanket tucking, they had not been this close physically. The couch was not large. It was one of those dainty, prissy things from the beginning of the century with legs that looked as if they might snap. The sort of the thing that was probably never meant to be sat on with both buttocks at the same time.

Anne placed her hands in her lap and tried not to think about his thigh barely six inches across the cushion from her own. It felt even closer. If one of them moved too quickly or breathed too deeply, would the seat give way and send them both to the floor?

The image caused a soft chuckle to escape her mouth, and thus she bore the wound of Lady Greville's gaze pricking at her with icy little needles. A moment later, however, those eyes were back to sewing a possessive border around J.P. Deverell, Esq., who seemed to do his best not to notice.

The footman arrived with the mulled wine, set a glass down beside Anne with an ungracious 'clack' and poured sloppily, spilling some on the polished wood table. He did not spill any when he poured the other two glasses.

"You have shown Mr. Deverell's coachman where he may sleep in the servants' quarters, I hope, William," Lady Greville demanded of her peevish footman.

"Yes." He squeezed out a sigh. "My lady."

"Then when you have shown Miss Foster to her room, you may retire to your own bed. I shall have no more need of you tonight. Wait by the door until Miss Foster is ready to go up." Evidently the lady was desirous for her absence too, as she had been for the unfortunate Lady Armstrong. The supposed friend, who had the audacity to grieve in her presence.

"Miss Follyot," the man beside her corrected their hostess again.

Anne looked at the full glass of wine that William had poured and left on the table along with the spilled puddles.

"Gracious, Miss Follyot, that is some very...earthy looking footwear," Lady Greville exclaimed.

Anne's gaze wandered to her feet and across at Lady Greville's dainty toes in their beribboned slippers. Earlier, the lady had worn riding boots over those slippers, but even her boots were of soft kid and clearly never worn in a very challenging environment for there was barely a mark on them. It still astonished her that other people could remain so pristine, like dolls in boxes. When Anne first arrived in London from Little Marshes, where there were no paved roads, she was startled by the noise of people, horses and carriages rumbling along the cobbled streets. She recalled her mother once telling her about a trip to town when *she* was a little girl and how folk had worn metal pattens over their shoes in bad weather, so that they clattered and clanged along the streets, sometimes causing sparks. Pattens were no longer in fashion, of course, but people still went to great lengths to avoid mud. They worried so much about dirt.

But then, Anne Follyot had never walked on fine carpet until she left her home and went out into the world. What did she know of possessing anything so expensive that never exposing it to dirt—to life or touch of any true kind— was more important than using it?

She squeezed her scruffily booted feet together and tried fitting them under the chair, away from the other lady's sneering glance.

"Miss Follyot grew up in the countryside among farms and fields," said Mr. Deverell. "Where people are accustomed to more practical footwear. Quite understandably."

Suddenly her fingers tingled. Anne quickly put her hands together in her lap, confused as to how and when they ever left that spot. She was sure that's where she'd left them the last time they came to her attention.

"Are you too hot, Miss Foster? You're very...red. Perhaps you are too close to the fire and should move to another seat. Over there."

"No, madam. I am comfortable."

Afraid that she was making an exhibit of herself, she reached for her glass goblet.

"The countryside, indeed? I thought her somewhat pastoral in appearance." The lady put on another false smile. "Charming, of course. One does get so very tired of fashion and making oneself a slave to it. Quite often one wishes it might be possible to throw it all aside and not care what one looks like. If only one did not have to go out to balls and parties."

"I have never been to a ball, or a large party," Anne confessed. "Only to our neighbors for cards and sherry at Christmas."

"Your family kept you out of society and the public eye, did they?" Lady Greville gave Deverell a sly look. "Most wise, I'm sure. Young girls these days often come out too soon. I myself was the victim of a hasty debut. My family wanted me well married and feared my looks would fade." She now stared hard at Anne. "Your family, it seems, had no need to worry about looks fading. And a young girl is far more prone to fortune hunters when she is plain. Too ready to be swept off her feet by the first man who flatters."

Anne had no idea about "coming out", "debuts" and men who flattered, other than what she had read in novels, so she drank her wine instead. The wine was heavily spiced and warm. It made her cough and then the man beside her murmured, "You need not drink it all, Miss Follyot. It might be too strong for you."

She looked askance. "Too strong? You have never tasted my father's home-made raspberry and dandelion wine, sir. I was raised on it as soon as I could walk."

His eyes narrowed. "That explains much. Even so, madam, I would advise caution. You ate very little dinner, remember, before you wanted to leave the tavern and drive on in haste?"

"Of course I remember," she exclaimed irritably. "I remember everything." *I am not a child. Do not treat me like one.* But she bit down on her tongue, for she had no one to blame but herself for his impression of her. He thought her a child because, in his eyes, she acted like one— admitting to the reading of novels, befriending mice and dancing about in snow before breakfast. Naturally he thought her foolish enough to forget herself with wine on a near-empty stomach, as if it might be her first taste of anything intoxicating. He did not want to be embarrassed by her in the company of his sophisticated "acquaintance."

But Mr. Deverell's solicitous attention to *her* sobriety seemed to make Lady Greville thirsty, for she called the footman back again from his exile at the edge of the room, clicking her fingers to have him pour another glass of wine for her. Then to go away again, only to call him back for another.

Anne understood now why the fellow was so ill-tempered, for the lady never once uttered a thank you and seemed to order him about just to watch him stride back and forth across the carpet in his begrudging step and tight livery.

"This is a very large house for one lady all alone, madam," Anne ventured, since her gentleman companion seemed reluctant to say anything more.

"Why should I not have it? I'm sure I earned it during the years of my marriage."

"Oh, I...I did not mean that you are not—"

"You sound like the baron's wretched daughters. The moment they found that their father had left the house and contents entirely to me, they protested that it ought to be sold and the profits divided between us. They even went so far as to claim I tricked their father into changing the will in my favor. That he was not in sound mind. They had no proof, of course. The signature was entirely genuine, and Arthur quite aware of what he did."

It occurred to Anne that the lady had drunk too much wine already that night, even before they met her. Up until now she'd hidden it well, but her cheeks were flushed and her eyes unfocused. Wilfred looked much the same when he'd imbibed too much and his temper was about to change from merry to maudlin and then argumentative.

"Besides," the lady went on, holding up her glass to study the rapidly decreasing contents, as if she thought there might be a crack in the crystal, "the ingrates are both married women now and have homes in which to live. Perfectly adequate homes. I daresay they would be happy to see me out on the street with nowhere to live."

"The sale of this house would surely have provided three handsome portions, madam," said Deverell. "In Mayfair you would not have been out on any street less than Grosvenor."

"However, the baron left it to me. His wife. The woman who put up with the decrepit old fool. I earned it."

Anne quickly finished her own glass of wine and shook her head when the footmen turned his step toward her.

"They resent me, of course," her ladyship continued. "Those girls were bitter and begrudging the moment I entered this house as a bride and usurped their father's love. I leave them to their self-pity. I was the victor, and they cannot stand it."

Anne was now so shocked that she had to speak. "I cannot imagine any woman would want to usurp a father's love for his daughters."

"You are young and know nothing of life. You have been sheltered at home by your family. But you will soon learn that a woman must fight for everything, every scrap, or else it will all be taken from her."

She set down her empty glass. "I may not know everything about life, madam, but I did have a father's love. I know that nothing could have changed that. Even if he had ever remarried after our mother died, I would have been happy for him. As long as the lady made him content. A husband's love is different to that of a father's, and there is room in a heart for many different kinds of love. I'm sure the Baron's daughters did not resent you."

"Oh, aren't you a little saint?"

"Indeed, no. I have been a horrid person at times. But I am willing to admit my mistakes and learn from them."

"I daresay you can afford to be so benevolent, if your father *loved* you so very much," she muttered spitefully. "The rest of us have a greater struggle."

"You speak of fighting for everything you have, Lady Greville, but surely as women we ought to stand together and fight, not to do battle against each other."

"That depends, my dear. Sometimes the enemy is another woman. To go through the world assuming they are all as sweetly naive as you and want nothing but peace is to underestimate your own sex."

Anne bit her tongue and smiled. "True, madam, I can only speak for myself. And as Mr. Deverell will tell you, I do that quite a lot. I have made his head ache with my chatter. I pray I do not distress you likewise."

The lady smiled in return, but without any pretence of warmth. Her teeth were gritted, her eyes hard, unmoved and uncaring. Then she turned to address Deverell, almost as if Anne had not spoken at all. Or else had committed another terrible faux pas that must be politely ignored for her own sake.

"J.P., do tell me, what is this mysterious business that keeps you so often in London and yet living a life away from society. Nobody seems to know anything about it."

He winced. "I prefer not to discuss business in the company of ladies. You would find it very tedious, and I'm sure Miss Follyot is tired."

They both looked at Anne, and she realized she was being dismissed. Like a child sent to bed so that the adults could speak in private. She'd had her treat— a glass of wine— and must now go up to the nursery with nanny.

Of course, next to Lady Greville, who was beautiful as a basket full of gilded lilies, elegant and fashionable, she looked like a silly lump of a girl. One who could not hold her tongue and her opinions for five minutes. He must be glad tonight of other, better company, and he would not want to suffer *her* rambling chatter any longer than necessary.

So she proudly bid them both a good evening and, with her chin up, followed the surly William to her room above.

Leave them to it. Why not? What did she care? All she needed was a good night's sleep and she would feel herself again, come the morning. She was a little shaky tonight, tired. At least here there was no possibility of running into Lizzie and Mr. Ingram and her adventure could continue.

Like the living space below, the bedchambers too were richly decorated, the bed in her room an enormous four-poster with carved Tudor roses, swathes of heavy tapestry and a step device required just to climb onto the mattress. She wondered if she ought to search for a pea under all the layers.

"Thank you, William," she said, with a warm smile. "I shall not put you to any further trouble."

He looked at her as if she'd insulted him with her gratitude. She'd heard that servants in grand houses could sometimes be more arrogant than their masters, and his gaze was just as hard and unfeeling as that of Lady Greville. A sneer curved his lips up and then down, as his nostrils widened and his pointy chin jabbed at her.

"This is not the best room in the house by far," he informed her coolly. "The best rooms are in the far wing. *This* is one of the worst rooms." Just in case she was in any doubt of her inferior status. Anne Follyot, of no fortune and no beauty.

"Really? Well, I think this one is splendid and certainly more luxurious than anything I've ever known," she replied cheerfully.

"Yes, she thought this would be sufficient for you."

Anne laughed softly. "No point casting pearls before swine."

He remained somber, glowering down his nose at her.

She added hastily. "This is far more than I deserve, to be sure."

With a stiff semi-bow, he turned to leave her.

"It's not haunted, is it?" she asked eagerly.

"Haunted?"

"Yes, by the old baron or one of his vengeful relatives who patrols the house nightly, looking for his own head, unaware that he holds it under his arm."

He sneered. "If there are ghosts here, I'm quite sure they'd leave you alone, madam. They'd have other bones to pick in this house."

With that he left her, closing the door with a long creak, a groan and a thud behind him.

Well, that put her in her place, she mused. Even the ghosts in this house would not think her worth haunting.

She walked around the room with her oil lamp, inspecting the draperies and the carved bed posts. Upon closer study one could see the worn patches, frayed edges and scratches. Thick cobwebs hung in the corners beneath the dusty canopy that stretched over the bed, and the wall paneling showed signs of woodworm. When she turned back the counterpane, the pungent odor of damp neglect rose up into her nostrils, so strong that she could taste it in the back of her throat. The pull bell beside the cold, dark fireplace hung loose, suggesting it would make no greater summons than a low clunk, should she try to ring for a servant. Perhaps the last soul who rang it did so in such terror and desperation that they broke it.

But there was nothing about ghosts to be feared. They had far more purpose than to drift about wailing; they simply needed somebody to listen and care.

Her bedchamber was a scene ripe for haunting, whatever the footman said, and yet she could conjure no excitement at the prospect, had no desire to imagine what might have happened there in the past. Tonight she was filled to the brim with new feelings. Perhaps her real life was finally more interesting than what she could imagine, and that was not because of this grand house, but because of the man below. The man who had sat beside her on a little couch, when there were many other chairs in the room from which to choose.

The man whose little finger had touched hers as they sat together.

That is what had made her own fingers tingle so suddenly— the shock of it, when his flesh brushed hers, where their hands had, somehow, come to rest on the silk cushion between them, in a space that was too narrow for both. She did not know whether it was accidental or deliberate.

Had their hostess seen that moment when Anne caught her breath and almost jumped off the cushions? Those cold eyes could take in any sight and never change their temperature.

But it left plain and simple Anne Follyot unnerved. She could not hide her feelings. And that was what he caused with only his little finger. Whatever would it feel like if he touched her with his whole hand one day? Or his lips?

She shook her head, amused at herself. He was hardly likely to kiss her, was he? Not thinking her a silly idiot, as he no doubt did.

He was not the first man who had touched her bare hand, but the first that startled her into this state of addled, cloth-headed confusion.

Well, if he thought her a silly, burbling idiot it was because he made her into one, she thought with a burst of irritation, shaking her fist at the shadows.

From now on she would not invest him with that amount of power over her thoughts and feelings. She would be aloof, like him, and not speak a single unnecessary word. If he wanted to know what she felt or thought about anything, he would have to force it out of her.

But she sat on the bed, her feet dangling from the great height, and her shoulders sagged.

It was obvious, even to a ninny like her, that there was some history between J.P. Deverell and Lady Greville, and it did not take a genius to know what it might contain. How could he enjoy the company of a woman like that?

Well, perhaps she was not always unkind and selfish. And she *was* remarkably beautiful. That could not be denied. The wine tonight must have made her seem more unpleasant than she truly was. Yes, on a normal evening, she was probably very nice, treated her servants well and was generous to her stepdaughters. They had simply caught Lady Greville on a bad day.

After all, he had fallen prey to Mrs. Marvington's talons too, every Thursday for a few weeks at least. The man couldn't get out of his own way, it seemed, when it came to women. Well, he was a Deverell. His path must be cluttered, fore and aft, with women of a certain scarlet hue.

Slipping on ice and landing at his feet.

A woman who only aspired to wings of rose madder silk, but who actually hid inside a brown caterpillar's skin, would be a poor alternative to one who knew what she was doing. A woman of experience.

J.P. Deverell, Esq. was quite within his rights to like anybody he chose.

None of this made Anne feel any more content. Concluding herself to be a wicked and unexpectedly jealous creature, she threw herself back onto the bed and then, sprawled there in a cloud of dust and floating mold spores, tried to think instead of her destination, of seeing her dear aunt again. Of Christmas. Lovely Christmas.

And of the fact that two days ago, she had never cared a jot about J.P. Deverell.

But it was very difficult to continue not caring when she kept, in her coat pocket, the little paper figure he had, quite unconsciously it seemed— while she chatted away about nothing and everything— made out of the folded tavern bill earlier that day.

It was almost an exact replica of the snow angel somebody made for her when she was five.

Chapter Twelve

The moment the door closed behind Anne, their hostess moved across the room to plant herself in the vacated seat beside him. He had no time to move away. Her hand hovered but a second in the air and then landed on his thigh, as she leaned closer, her wine-scented breath brushing his face.

"What great fortune that I should come upon you this evening, J.P. Fate was on my side for once."

"It is good of you to give us shelter, madam."

"Come now, you know my name. You may as well call me by it now that we are alone."

He sighed. "Maria, I did not come here to—" He stopped the progress of her hand with his own. "Please do not embarrass us both."

She drew back, a low gasp shuddering out of her mouth. It was almost, but not quite, a laugh. The breath was too cold for that.

"I do not wish for there to be any confusion again," he said carefully, "so I had better speak plainly. There can be no question of anything like that between us, not tonight, or at any point in the future."

"I thought you sent the girl out so that we could be alone."

"I did not think it proper for her to hear this."

"Hear what? You mean to talk and waste this perfect opportunity? That is not like you at all."

"I am a different man now, Maria."

"So I see," she breathed, inching even closer. "You were a fine young man the last time you came to me, talented, but a little too intense and restless. Now perhaps you are matured, relaxed into your skin and not in such haste to leave a lady's bed— or go to it. We can try again. Mend our fences."

"Again you misunderstand me, madam. When I said I am a different man, I meant that I am more content with myself than I was four years ago when I came to your bed. I did not know then what I wanted."

"Do you know now?"

"That is... uncertain. But I know what I do *not* want."

Her cheeks sucked in, and she slithered back against the other arm of the couch. "Then tell me what you are about with that odd creature."

"Odd creature?"

"The dumpling with whom I catch you, in the most unlikely act of gallantry, traveling across the country in the depths of winter. I did think it strange to see you with such an ordinary, unfashionable creature, and you were never the sort to put yourself out for anybody. And then I realized— she must be rich. Very rich. A homely heiress in farmer's boots? Where on earth did you find her?"

That was how little she knew or understood him— to imagine he would pursue a woman for money.

"She found me, actually," he replied. "Or her trunk did. I tripped over it."

And as he spoke those words, he suddenly remembered a story his mother once told him, of how True Deverell stumbled over her, when she worked in her father's law office and the man came in to discuss his scandalous divorce.

"*Get out of my blasted way,* were your father's first words to me," she'd told him with a chuckle. "It was three o'clock on a Tuesday. I remember it as clear as if it were yesterday. He was in such a foul-tempered hurry that we collided and he knocked papers out of my hands. When I stooped to pick them up he stepped over me, barely even looking at me. I thought to myself, *that's where men like True Deverell go wrong. They don't notice me. The mutton-head would not know a decent woman if he tripped over her.*"

Now their son had tripped over Miss Follyot, a decent woman he had not noticed for too long.

Meanwhile, Lady Greville laughed, the sound hard and sharp, piercing his thoughts. "You tripped over her trunk and rather than bite off her head, you indulge in this pretense of gentlemanly valor? So I was right; she is rich, and light in the head. How fortunate that you discovered her. Do her family even know you have her in your clutches? You Deverells have always been opportunists."

"I told you, madam, I take her to her aunt. Her finances are not my concern." Or yours, he might have said, but he was actually trying to be polite. Practicing. For what he did not know. But his mother would be pleased.

"As soon as she began to talk so glowingly of her dead father, I understood. He left her a vast fortune, of course, but she has been sheltered and cosseted, hidden away in the countryside. She has never been 'out'. Now you mean to pluck the poor creature from the virginal vine and make her— and her fortune— yours, before she knows the danger she is in."

"Madam, you leap to extraordinary conclusions."

"You're a Deverell. You must want something that she has, and it certainly is not beauty. There must be something in it for you."

He thought about it for a moment. "Her company."

"That plain, unrefined girl?"

"Indeed, I find Miss Follyot quite extraordinary and anything but plain."

"Thus you defend her to me. How very quaint. Jacob Dockery always said you were an old-fashioned gentleman at heart, but I never believed it."

J.P. stood and bowed. "Good evening, Lady Greville. You must excuse me. It's been a long day, and I have far yet to travel. Perhaps the footman would be so good as to show me to a room."

She stared up at him, her eyes drooping at the corners, puzzled. "I hope her fortune makes it worth your while. I ought to take her aside and warn her. The poor, stupid creature."

"The young lady has my measure already, but by all means take her aside. I think you'll find that the treasure in her possession is not the sort that can pay your bills. But I have no doubt she'd be happy to share some of it with you. At length."

Half-inebriated, the lady blinked and looked confused.

He said nothing more and left the room.

There was a strange excitement careening through his body, a restlessness. He took the stairs four at a time and very nearly whistled a tune.

* * * *

Anne sat up when she heard a tap at her door. Her first thought was that the old baron had come to see who slept there and warn her off the premises. But then she heard a soft, deep voice.

"Miss Follyot?"

She climbed down from the bed and took her oil lamp to the door. "Who is it?" she demanded primly.

A pause and then a slightly exasperated, "I suppose I could be any one of the twenty men likely to be at your bedchamber door in this house, in the middle of the night."

"You could be a robber."

"Who, having found his way into the house in some sly, clandestine manner, now goes to the trouble of knocking on your door."

"Well, if you put it like that—"

"Do not open your door. That is not necessary, madam. I merely wanted to let you know that should you require anything, I am across the corridor."

"And why might I require anything in the night? What might I require from *you* in particular, sir?"

She heard a deep sigh. "Nothing, to be sure."

"Is it another mouse from which you need me to defend you?" she asked cheekily.

"Good night, madam."

Anne forgot her intention to be aloof and opened her door, peering around it to see him walking away into the room opposite her own.

"Why are you here?" she whispered. "This is the worst part of the house. The footman assured me of it. I assumed you would be given a chamber in the better wing, free of mold and drafts." *In reach of Lady Greville's caresses.*

He swung around, lifting his own lamp to find her face. "I was. The room and the terms of use were unsatisfactory." His cravat was untied, a lock of hair falling over his brow.

"Oh." She swallowed. "How did you know where I was?"

"William informed me when I objected to the room I was given."

"Lady Greville will not be happy at the rearrangement."

He gave a sort of smile. "William will manage the lady's disappointment. I suspect it is a duty that falls often to him."

Once she'd had a moment to think about what he suggested, Anne was shocked. "The footman?"

"These things happen, Miss Follyot. Not only in novels." He bowed his head, gave a sly smirk, turned and took his lamp into the room across the corridor. "You need not have opened your door in a state of undress. Go back inside before any harm befalls you."

"Any harm?" She'd actually forgotten she was barefoot and clad only in her nightgown.

"You could catch cold. It is not safe to be wandering the corridors...like that. In a strange house."

"Why? What might become of me?"

He stopped again, turning back to face her. "Any manner of things."

"Perhaps I feel better out here, talking to you," she whispered, "than inside that room."

He tilted his head. "I'm sure I shall regret asking, but why is that, Miss Follyot?"

"It's haunted, you know. My room."

"Haunted? By whom?"

"I cannot say." She shivered, and her breath formed a cloud of warm mist in the cold air. "But he's very old, has holes in his socks and grey hair growing out of his ears. It might be the ghost of my future husband."

"You mean, Mr. Darkwinters of Basingstoke, Egypt and the Argentine. And Wales?"

She scowled. "I told you that because you were being remarkably presumptuous about my state as a woman of... singularity."

"You're certainly that." His lip quirked. "I can assure you, Miss Follyot, you are safer in the custody of ghosts— even that of your future husband, whoever he might be— than with the flesh and blood residents of this house at night. Specters can do you less harm."

"Do you speak from experience?" Of course he did. Why else had he come to this wing, instead of staying on Lady Greville's "better" side of the house?

He stood looking at her for a moment.

With her free hand she gathered up the ruffled collar of her nightgown.

"I have not led a life so sheltered that I cannot see what she was to you before," she added on another trembling cloud of breath. "You need not conceal it from me. She did not."

"You think that is the only reason why I changed my room?"

"Is it?"

"Miss Follyot, you might not balk at telling strangers everything about yourself, whether true or constructed by an overly-active imagination. I, however, prefer not to open my life like a bag of looted candlesticks to be picked over by every Tom, Dick and Harry pawnbroker I come upon."

"But we're not strangers now, surely."

"I had not realized my private affairs became your business simply because we are sharing a carriage ride together."

"Well, of all the bold-faced cheek! I know it is not—"

"I did not want you to be afraid or think yourself alone in this part of the house. I'm sure that you, a modern, independent young woman, will scoff at the idea, but I consider myself responsible for your welfare on this journey and feel it incumbent upon me to watch over you. That is why I changed my room."

Her fingers loosened their grip on her nightgown. "Oh. That's not very Deverell-like."

"I know." He shrugged. "It does not have the air of me about it, but apparently I care for your comfort."

"Oh," she said again, quite at a loss for once.

"I think these uncustomary thoughts of kindness with which you currently burden me have something to do with the hole in your hat ribbon."

She groaned. "You were not supposed to see that."

"Alas, you are unaccomplished in the art of concealment. But I admire the effort of adornment. Particularly the seasonal flair."

"Well, a girl ought to make an effort, if she's embarking on adventure with a scandalous Deverell."

"I can assure you, very few women bother. You're something of an oddity in my experience." He gave a wry little smile. "Not an unpleasant one."

"*At least I know there is something that entertains you then,*" she had said to him earlier that day.

"*Yes. You do.*"

Did he mean that yes, she knew there was something? Or did he mean that she, Anne Follyot of Little Marshes, amused him? Such a small sentence made magnificent with promise when uttered in his deep voice. Whatever it meant, it meant the world to her.

"Go back inside your chamber, Miss Follyot," he urged, taking a backward step into his own room. "Sweet dreams. As you say."

When he spoke those words in his low, gruff voice, they did not sound at all like the innocent suggestion they ought to be. His door shut.

Anne walked up to it with her oil lamp in hand. *Mr. Deverell, I think I remember you now. From all those years ago.* But the words would not come. Unusually for her. She could not bring herself to tell him about the Snow angel. She was still hoping he would remember it himself, without her prompting.

She closed her eyes and willed with all her heart. *Remember me. See me as I see you.*

From inside his room she heard the sound of buttons hitting wood and boot soles falling to the floor. She opened her eyes and swallowed, thinking of his cravat tossed aside, revealing the broad, strong column of his throat. Then his shirt tugged off over his head. She imagined the muscles in his back and arms, lit by oil lamp, as he stretched and groaned.

Her heart was thumping very hard and fast.

"I am sorry I made us ride on tonight," she blurted suddenly through the door.

"Think nothing of it," he replied, slightly breathless. "We are both eager to be done with this journey. It was not your fault that the next inn was full. At least you are not with child and riding a donkey. Could be worse, as you like to say."

The sound of more clothing thrown to a chair.

"Mr. Deverell, I am not eager to be done with it. Not at all."

Silence.

"I know I should pretend otherwise, but I cannot. I do not want my adventure to be over."

The door opened abruptly, and she caught her breath.

He was barefoot, in his breeches and shirt, which hung loose around his thighs. Her imagination had got ahead of itself, alas, for he was not so far into his disrobing as she'd pictured. "Then why insist on riding onward today?" he demanded. "For the life of me I shall never understand women."

"I do have a very good reason, but it is not that I want to arrive at our destination any sooner. Quite the opposite."

His eyes slowly lightened, as if clouds lifted, but there remained a note of wariness.

"I... enjoy your company," she blurted. "Sir."

He stared.

"I should not admit it so readily, should I? I'm sure it's very forward."

After a moment, he said, "I think we might dispense with the *sir* then, don't you?"

She nodded eagerly, lips pressed together before they might say anything else they shouldn't contemplate.

He stepped forward, took her oil lamp and set it down on the floor. "You are intent on catching cold. Is that your plan to delay us?"

She shook her head, feeling as if she might burst.

He placed his hands around her face. "Go to bed. Anne." And then, as if it was the most natural thing in the world, he bent his head and kissed her. On her trembling lips.

Anne could not say how long it lasted. Somehow it reached inside, down through her veins taking all the nervousness out of her and replacing it with warmth, confidence. And bold desire. She had once tasted hot chocolate and thought that nothing else would ever be better. It was, she knew now, an incorrect assumption.

Even when his mouth was gone again, she could still feel the imprint it had left upon her lips. "Is that entirely proper?" she murmured, slightly dazed, wide awake and very hot.

"I'm a Deverell," he replied smugly. "What did you expect? We do things...differently."

"I should be shocked."

"If you are not, then I didn't do it right."

So he kissed her again and she closed her eyes, leaning into him, lifted up on her toes. Her skin tingled, every inch of it melting like snow before a good fire. His fingertips whispered through her hair, stroked her cheek.

Stepping back, hands falling to his sides, he said gruffly, "All part of the adventure, Anne Follyot. No extra charge."

"We shall look after each other then, in this side of the house."

He scratched his chest through his shirt and belatedly seemed to remember his lack of proper clothing. "Go to bed. We'll start early tomorrow and be on our way. I don't want to stay here longer than necessary, for obvious reasons." Again he shut the door.

But something told her he still stood there on the other side of it and had not moved away.

"Very well then," she called through the door. On a halting breath, she added, "If you should find yourself awoken by ghouls and phantoms, sir, feel free to knock at my door. We shall fight off the undead together in this side of the house where they inevitably wander. I am not afraid of them and, in fact, feel some affinity with the lost souls caught between heaven and earth."

"You will be the first person I call upon, madam, should the need ... or anything else...arise. Now go to bed, before I am obliged to pick you up and carry you bodily to it."

Oh. Would he? A most interesting vision to ponder. She clasped her hands together.

"Anne! Bed." It sounded as if he'd just stubbed his toe. Certainly he was in pain of some kind.

She took up her oil lamp and, as if sleep-walking, Anne returned to her room and her bed.

This time her mood was improved considerably. Not that her descent into sleep was aided at all. She might not be prone to sickness, but his kiss had definitely left her feverish and restless.

He had kissed her. Twice. Threatened to carry her in his arms to bed. Her bed. But, still...

She was on her way to a frock of that luscious silk rose madder, and no mistake.

Chapter Thirteen

The next morning Anne was up before him and at breakfast already when he came down. It was evident that she had got her breath back after their tiring day yesterday, and now she regaled a grey, weary and pinch-faced hostess with tales of her life in London.

"I was telling Lady Greville about my post at Lockreedy and Velder," she exclaimed, beaming. "She does not approve of young ladies working either."

J.P. was filling his plate from the dishes on the sideboard and made no comment.

"I suppose she also thinks I would be safer with my aunt in Widecombe," she added.

He looked over his shoulder at her and was struck by how pretty she looked that morning. Far prettier than she ought. Even with that saucy tongue bulging in her cheek as her eyes laughed at him.

"You would be safe from men like Deverell," said Lady Greville, smug. "It seems you haven't been sufficiently warned of certain dangers. Has nobody explained to you, my dear girl, the wickedness of men?"

"Oh, I know how dreadful they can be, your ladyship. I have an older brother."

"That is not quite—"

"He always stole the best conkers from my collection and claimed them as his own. He also ate jam and honey directly from the jars stored in the pantry and when the loss was discovered blamed it on me."

"Yes, but I refer to other men—"

"Rakes, rogues and seducers?"

"Precisely."

"Oh, I never seem to be of interest to that sort of man. I think it's the brown."

"The brown?"

"I was always told it would do for me and one should never try to be something one isn't. But occasionally I cannot help wondering if my life would have been a little more exciting in other colors."

It was most amusing watching this exchange and Lady Greville's attempts to follow along. "I did not know you had a brother. I was under the impression that you were an only child, my dear."

"No. I am the middle child of three."

"I see."

J.P. realized she was now recalculating, dividing that vast fortune she'd imagined between three.

But Anne was now in full steam, showing their hostess her boots, explaining about the special waterproof socks and her purpose for the invention. Her conversation followed no rules, took no particular order. For Lady Greville, accustomed to more fashionable modes of bored dialogue that followed an established pattern of coldly polite trivia, it must be quite a shock to find herself engaged in this lively exchange.

Anne Follyot was a remarkable creature. She almost made *him* believe that something magic was at work. That anything might be possible.

Last night, when she peered around her door at him, he had the surprise treat of seeing her dark hair loose about her shoulders. It was longer, thicker and curlier than he had imagined. Today it was back in its usual knot, but the vision of how she looked last night stayed with him, lit by the soft glow of an oil lamp. He saw again her cheeks gently flushed, her eyes shining with curiosity, the rumpled white collar of her nightgown, framing her chin and neck, the skin of her slender throat bared to his gaze as he watched her swallow. Her eyes were large and dark, her lips the soft pink of a small rosebud, newly unfurling on a damp spring morning. He pictured his fingertip carefully tracing that sweeping bow, parting her lips with his thumb. Her lashes fanned slowly down and up. His fingers left her warm lips and trailed downward, stroking that neck, sliding under the linen collar to feel the heat of her; the reckless, unsteady drum of her heart, seeking out and holding that firm, delectable—

"Damn and blast!" He'd crushed a bread roll in his hand, dropped it, and in his clumsy attempt to catch it again, knocked a chafing dish of kedgeree all over the sideboard.

"William can clean it up," Lady Greville grumbled. Her elbow propped up on the table, she rested her hand against her forehead, clearly suffering the effects of too much mulled wine and Miss Follyot so early in the morning. "It is the one thing he's good for."

J.P. took a seat at the table, deciding to forgo food after all. Blood surged through his body and a thin layer of perspiration coated his skin, as if he'd just ridden in a horse race and won. By accident. He could not have eaten, even if he was hungry.

He stared at Anne Follyot. Where had he been all these years without her face before him, without her voice in his ear? The women he knew before were statues, standing under dust sheets in a lost room of his memory, and Anne Follyot ran around pulling off all the covers, bringing light and fresh air into his thoughts. She was unavoidably in his present. In his path. Like that trunk.

Oh, but he did not want to feel this way. He did not want complications in his life. Unpredictability. Mess.

Too much bloody happiness. A man who felt that way was destined for a great and painful fall. Not everybody could be like his father and land on his lucky feet with a soul mate.

He should never have kissed her last night.

But he was a Deverell and she would have been disappointed if he did not.

Would not want to let her down, would he?

"You look as if you need coffee," said his hostess, reaching an unsteady hand to pour it. "I do hope you slept well," she added, in a tone which suggested her greatest desire was for the opposite.

"I did. Thank you, madam. I found a bed in the east wing most comfortable after William mistakenly took me to another that was surely too fine for me."

Maria glared at him and then returned to Anne, who was clearly too fascinating a puzzle to be left undone for long. "I am shocked you need to earn a living, my dear."

"I want to live as independently as I am able, your ladyship, and not rely on others to keep me."

"But you will marry, surely."

"Only if I find the right toad, your ladyship."

"I beg your pardon?"

Anne chuckled. "Rather than rush into a marriage to anybody, I should like to see more of the world myself and enjoy some adventure, before I am constrained by the bonds of matrimony."

"Is there any bond that could constrain you, I wonder?" he muttered.

Maria leaned back in her chair and groaned. "You waste your time, young woman. Trust me. There is nothing good in the world to see, and adventures are vastly over-rated. Take this warning from one who has known a great many...adventures. This world is a harsh, unforgiving place to one who does not follow the rules."

"But there must be—"

"Life is war and cruelty and deceit."

"There is also art and love and beauty. There are folk who help, who strive to make the world a better place. I prefer not to dwell on the bleak. After all, as my father used to say, there would be no such thing as darkness, if there was not also light."

"Good lord, you make my skull ache. Are you always so relentlessly happy?"

"To be content makes less demands on my purse."

Feigning preoccupation with his coffee for now J.P. stayed out of the debate. He realized that some sound must have escaped his mouth for he felt Maria's gaze slip sideways to watch him curiously again. He cleared his throat and reached for the sugar bowl. When the little silver tongs fell to the table with a clatter, he quickly tossed five cubes into his cup with his unusually unsteady fingers.

"One day, Miss Foster," said Maria, "your best, most fruitful years will be behind you and all the better men snapped up. Of course since you have no need of money, you feel no haste yet. But in your desire to be independent, you will find yourself superfluous to society, an old maid."

"A grievous prospect, indeed." She was somber for a moment— a rare occurrence and unlikely. Then, having paused a moment, as if in due reflection of her sorry plight, she resumed her cheerful pace of thought. "But a risk I am willing to take, your ladyship. As a female, many choices have been forbidden me. But as a woman of almost two and twenty, with no parent living, and no male relative yet eager to take control of me, at least the decision of whom I may marry and when, or even if, is within my power. So, all things considered, it could be worse."

Maria pursed her lips and began to shake her head, until she apparently remembered how it throbbed. "I cannot decide, Miss Follyot, whether you are the most irritating or the most guileless creature I have ever met."

"But at least you remember my name now."

* * * *

At the front door, Anne thanked Lady Greville for her hospitality and was rewarded with a limp half-smile.

"Your company was...interesting, young woman. I doubt we'll meet again. Such a pity."

The lady's goodbye to Deverell was even colder, but with just a tinge of regret.

"I hope one day she learns to enjoy her fine house and all the lovely things in it," said Anne, waving enthusiastically through the carriage window as they rolled away into the snow. "It seems a tragedy that she, a beautiful woman, must live there all alone, discontent, yet surrounded by lovely treasures."

"You are more generous to her than she was to you."

"Just because she does not like me now, does not mean she never will. You did not like me at first, and now we are the best of friends."

"You are irrepressibly sanguine," he muttered, bewildered.

"But she will be sorry if we do not meet again. She said so."

He looked at her sternly. "Anne, I fear you—"

Then she laughed heartily. "Your face is a picture, sir. I may be a country girl from Little Marshes, but we have sarcasm there too. It is not exclusive to you clever, refined, well-shod folk in town."

His lips pressed together tightly, his eyes studying her, unblinking. They were an odd color, something between lilac and silver and smoke. She had never seen eyes that color, changing like a bellwether for his temper. Lovely might not be the right word to describe them, however; magnificent would do better. Terrifyingly awe-inspiring. Once they had looked at her, she never wanted them to look away again and was jealous of anything they perused instead.

All night she had pondered her paper snow angel and Deverell's kiss. Two gifts he'd given to her, sixteen years apart, both had left a deep and lasting impression.

She remembered the vicarage party now. It was like opening the pages of an old book in her mind and there was the picture, slowly drawn and coming magically to life. A whirling tempest of snow obscured everything for a moment, but then it came to settle over the scene, lit by a shower of sparking stars, flying glittering ice crystals that gave her back just a moment in time while they glowed their brightest— how she had cried after the snowball hit her in the face and he, a boy who seemed so tall and somber, took the time to cheer her up by folding the page of blank white paper torn from a book. Swiftly his long fingers worked with the paper and she, forgetting her tears, watched enthralled as the snow angel came to life.

"Don't cry. I hate to see girls cry. Here, the angel will look after you and make sure that you are safe." His voice was low, a little awkward, not wanting to be heard by others perhaps, not liking to show softness or tenderness.

Then the image was gone, the ice sparkles melting into the fallen snow, their light snuffed.

It left her heart aching, but for what? For the past? For herself and what she might never find in the future?

Or for the man sitting across from her now, in the present? The sad fellow he had become. At least he looked a little less burdened that morning.

Remember me. Remember the snow angel. See me as I see you. She desperately tried to work her way into his head. But he must remember on his own, without her prompting, otherwise she would never know whether he truly remembered, or whether he simply said he did. He made those paper sculptures quickly and thoughtlessly, the way some people bit their nails or drummed with their fingers. It was unconsciously done, apparently.

But her angel was special. He must remember it, surely.

How long did they have left together on this journey? She still had a lot of work to do, if his frown was to be chased away completely, and she did not like to leave a job half undone.

All she knew was that he had to remember on his own. He must.

It was as if he would save her life by remembering.

He had not mentioned his kiss today, and she could not raise the subject. Usually she would, but when one was trying to impress a man with composure and maturity, one really shouldn't let him know that one little kiss had such an affect. Or even two. *Good gracious no, it happens to one all the time.*

Who knew why he had done it? He was a Deverell; they did not wait for permission, or follow rules. In all likelihood he had thought nothing of it. He might even have kissed her last night just to shut her up, she mused.

"Do you think we will come to the end of our journey by the end of the day?" she asked.

"Perhaps. If the road is fast and there are no more delays."

She sighed. "I almost invited Lady Greville to my aunt's house for Christmas. It seems so awful that she is in that big house all alone."

"Do not concern yourself. The lady is capable of finding company when she requires it."

"And I don't suppose I could have persuaded her to come. It would not be her sort of function. My aunt lives simply and quietly."

"Considering Lady Greville thinks you're an heiress escaped from a lunatic asylum, I very much doubt she might have been prevailed upon to travel with you," he muttered. Before she could say anything, he added wryly, "I am only with you, she believes, because you are my hapless prey for some purpose too awful to mention."

"She must read novels too. See? I knew she and I could be friends after all and you doubted it." She laughed and then frowned. "I did wonder why she kept saying that money was no object for me. What made her think me an heiress?"

"When you spoke of your father's love."

"I don't understand."

"For a lady like Maria Greville, love can only mean money. She has no appreciation of anything else. Her cause is always mercenary. For her there must always be something gained or else it is not worth her time. You spoke fondly of your father and so she assumed he left you with a fortune." He paused. "I notice you did not tell her about your explorer fiancé in Basingstoke."

"I did not think she would be impressed."

"And I would?"

"You believed it for a moment, did you not? Admit it, J.P.!"

"Madam, I was never in any doubt that the man capable of splicing himself to you with an engagement must be the bravest adventurer in the land. But I did not think such a man could yet have been born."

She laughed at that, and he looked as if he would too. Almost.

But suddenly there was a crack, a bang, a thud and their progress ground to a shuddering halt.

* * * *

The Snow Angel

The axle was broken.

Jarvis was obliged to ride onward with one of the horses and fetch assistance.

"I must apologize, Anne. This will delay our journey."

"These things do happen, J.P. It is, I understand, a likelihood of travel."

"All part of the adventure?"

She nodded.

He gave her an arch look. "You didn't, by chance, break this axle yourself, did you?"

"Yes, I crept downstairs last night while you all slept and I took an axe to it. I confess it was most satisfying."

"Something left you with an excess of energy and restlessness, did it?"

"Did it leave *you* the same?"

He turned away and resumed his pacing. There, indeed, was her answer.

At least it was not presently snowing and the stone on the verge proclaimed the nearest village to be only a mile ahead, so it should not take Jarvis long to return with able hands and tools.

Anne remained under her blanket, while he paced beside the crippled vehicle and reassured the other horses. She had started to feel very limp and sad. Their journey was coming to an end.

He had not remembered.

It had all been for nothing.

The cold crept up her legs, tightened the breath in her lungs.

"Aha! I see another carriage approaching," he shouted, rubbing his gloved hands together, shoulders lifted against the harsh wind.

She peered out, saw Mr. George Ingram's ginger whiskers and immediately felt her heart sink to her toes. Well, that was that.

There was now no escaping her sister and the horror of rescue.

* * * *

He was curious. Why had she pretended not to know them before? J.P. recognized the young couple from the tavern yesterday, when Anne had been in such haste to leave. Now she was forced to introduce them.

"Mr. Deverell, this is my sister, Elizabeth, and her husband, Mr. George Ingram."

Her sister was small and fair, very well dressed, pretty in an ordinary way. Dashing forward, she clasped Anne's hands and exclaimed, "What could you be thinking not to wait for us? When we got to the boarding house on Thursday, your landlady told us you had already gone. Imagine our surprise! Of course you must come with us now. Mustn't she, George?"

With his own vehicle temporarily useless, J.P. could not put up any argument. More snow could well be on its way and Anne, he agreed solemnly, would be better off joining her sister.

While her trunk was being transferred, he heard her telling the other woman how J.P. Deverell had been commissioned by their aunt for the journey to Widecombe.

"I am sure he will happy to go on alone without my company," she said. "I have troubled him enough."

Thus this strange odyssey was abruptly over.

"I shall wish you a merry Christmas, J.P., whether you approve the sentiment or not." And she reached out her hand, as she did two nights ago.

This time he held it properly and lifted it to his lips rather than shake it. With his heels pressed together, he bowed over her fingers. "Miss Anne Follyot. It has been most enlightening."

"You will go home now, won't you? To see your family? You've come this far, after all."

"Yes, and I shall tell them that you are to blame for it."

"I've been to blame for much worse things." She climbed up into her brother-in-law's carriage, the door closed, and she opened the sash window. "Now you know why I wanted to ride on ahead yesterday," she whispered. "You must think me a grievous maladroit for putting you to all this trouble, when I could simply have waited for my sister in London."

Yes, it was odd that she threw in her lot with him, instead of waiting for her sister. He would not even try to make sense of it. "I shall assume your wickedness to be the fault of winter's early darkness and boredom. I hear it's something that happens to young ladies this time of year."

"Shall we ever meet again, do you suppose?" She sounded forlorn, he thought, his pulse quickening.

"I should think it inevitable."

"Oh." Her face brightened, only to fall again. "You mean to say that I shall turn up in your life again, like a bad penny? As I have done so many times without being noticed."

"I meant, Anne, that there is little doubt that we shall run into each other again—since you work for me."

She stared. Her lips parted, eyes widened.

"And you are fortunate, perhaps, that I am not an elderly Scotsman in a kilt. Tumbling over your trunk in the street might have had more severe consequences and led to more complaints than it did."

The horses pulled away and her sister, protesting the draft, leaned over to shut the window.

He laughed then, as he had not laughed in a long time. She probably heard it, even above the cantering hooves.

* * * *

Anne would have liked to sit quietly with her thoughts, but that luxury was not to be. Lizzie was exceedingly curious, of course, and wanted to know all about J. P. Deverell.

"I can tell you little," Anne replied. "He's a very private gentleman." He was her employer. He was "Mr. Lockreedy", the mysterious recluse. The scoundrel! The rogue!

He had kissed her. Twice.

"But fancy our aunt leaving you to the hands of a *Deverell*, sister. Anything could have happened in his company!"

"Yes." She sighed wistfully. "Couldn't it?"

Her sister did not seem to hear her replies at all.

"Seemed like a nice enough fellow," George ventured.

"Yes, but a *Deverell*!"

Anne's head ached. She tried to rub her temple and ease the pain, but her arm felt oddly stiff and would not oblige.

"George and I only just decided, last month, to visit Aunt Follyot for Christmas, did we not, George?" her sister continued. "She wrote such a lovely letter to me when we married and sent me some exquisite lace. I said to George, we really ought to visit Aunt Follyot at Christmas."

Not a thought for any other arrangement or company that lady might have had.

"She would not ask us, to be sure, for she would imagine Mr. Ingram and I to be very busy and engaged socially, I suppose. You, of course, would have nothing else to do, so it is no wonder she thought of asking you, Anne. She knew you would be all alone and have no engagements whatsoever." Lizzie said all this out loud, sorting through explanations for the aunt asking Anne for Christmas and not her. "It is just a surprise that she would ask a Deverell to take you to her. Well, she is an old lady and perhaps does not have all her faculties. In any case, now we shall surprise her together! What fun!"

Anne was once again the object of pity for her family. But what did it matter? She had made Mr. J.P. Deverell laugh, and she had caused him to go home for Christmas.

That was quite an achievement for Anne Follyot of Little Marshes and a lot of brown.

Oh, but her head hurt. Why could she not move her arms? She tried again to stretch out her fingers, wishing she had his hand in hers. So strong and firm and safe.

But he was not there. She had done all that she could, but he would not come to her until he remembered the Snow angel.

She felt terribly bruised, every inch of her.

Remember me.

Remember your Snow angel.

Chapter Fourteen
Roscarrock Castle 1877

"How lovely to have you here," said his mother, teary-eyed, but valiantly holding back the drips. "My darling J.P., I knew you would not let me down."

"Don't get excited just yet, mama. I'm afraid I did not deliver Miss Follyot to her aunt." Chagrinned he explained about her sister interrupting their journey. "It seems your friend was unaware of her other niece's intentions to visit, or else I would never have been engaged for the task."

"Oh, well, at least you got her half way." His mother patted his shoulder and then his ear, in a strange, distracted way. "And in one piece?"

"I left her quite intact. Perhaps, however," he smirked, "rather more speechless than customary."

"But how did you find poor, little Anne? Much changed?"

"Not so little anymore." He smirked. "Rounded out in all the proper and improper places."

"John Paul!"

He always liked to shock his mother. Surprised, in fact, that anything still could shock her. "But then a woman of one and twenty is bound to be changed from what she was at five, mama."

"Yes, of course." She studied his face. "You did remember her then."

"Eventually."

"I am glad. Dear little Anne. She has had such a hard life, looking after her family since she was but a slip of a thing."

"She seems remarkably cheerful and content despite that."

His mother tucked her arm under his. "And you look happy yourself, J. P. Much more relaxed than the last time I saw you."

"Do I?"

"Yes, there is a gleam in your eye that I have never before seen there. Not for many years, at least."

"Hmm. Well, it's Christmas. I am reliably informed that miracles do happen at such times. Even to the likes of me."

She kissed his cheek. "I hope so, my darling."

"Mother, I am too old to be fussed over."

"Only by me, I suspect."

That night he dreamed of Anne with her aunt and sister, sipping tea by the fire, telling them all an outrageous story about her journey through the snow. He saw it all clearly, as it must surely be, every detail— holly on the mantle and pine cones lending their sweet scent to the air, cakes on the sideboard and a grandfather clock in the corner, gently clicking through the minutes.

He saw Anne glance up at the clock face and knew that she wondered where he was now, what he did.

But wait— her eyes were closed, as if she'd suddenly fallen asleep. The tea cup spilled from her hand, and the other two women jumped to their feet as a stain spread across the carpet.

The room looked different now, darker and more sinister. The grandfather clock had no face, and the pendulum had ceased to swing.

Anne stood in the middle of the room, her hands over her face.

He felt a cold chill.

If only there was some way to reach a person over that distance. He concentrated very hard on the shape of her ear and the quick pulse beating away behind it. He whispered.

I remember you now. How did I ever forget? How did I not see you before?

He raised a hand to the side of her neck, finding the loose lock of hair that hung there in a spiral, twisting in the breeze of his whisper.

"Anne," said her aunt's voice, "you are so far away, my dear. Come back to us. Come back to us."

She shook her head, both hands still covering her face. It was late and she was tired, but she wanted them to know he was a good man, so she took out her paper snow angel, unfolded her wings, and set her there to tell them how it happened that J.P. Deverell once showed a little girl his gentle side.

He whispered the story into her ear, and she echoed it with tears trapped under her eyelids.

* * * *

1861

The snowball, thrown by her brother, hit her soundly on the side of her head, just by her eye. J.P. saw it happen and was appalled. The little girl fell into a snow heap and howled, her face red, one pudgy hand clasped to her temple.

Her brother ran off, playing with the other children.

"You'd better come inside." J.P. lifted her to her feet, brushed the snow from her coat, checked that she was not seriously hurt and then held her hand. "Don't cry."

The adults were in the parlor, and he knew there would be a great deal of shrieking and fussing if he took her in there while she still sobbed. Instead he took her into the vicar's study and found some paper. It was the only thing he could think of to take her mind off the sting.

"See? She's an angel. Here are her wings."

The little girl gazed up at him, her eyes huge and wet, still rubbing her head with one hand, but no longer making a noise.

"What's your name then?" he asked.

"Angel," she said. "I'm an angel." She held out her arms. "Here are my wings."

"That's right. You're an angel."

She sniffed, wiped her nose on her sleeve and then reached up to take the paper doll from his hand.

"You're a snow angel," he said and smiled, reaching down to ruffle her dark, damp curls. "Don't tell anybody I made you that." It was not the sort of thing a boy like him ought to do. The other boys would make fun of him, because he cared when a girl cried.

But he'd only just discovered that weakness in himself and it was not the sort of thing expected of a Deverell.

"*Takes after his mother*," his father often said. But J.P. wanted to be like his father too. True Deverell was a legend. He surely did not go around making paper angels for little girls who cried.

So he did not think of it again. The paper folding was simply a habit for his restless fingers. It was not important.

The Snow Angel

Except to the girl whose name he never learned.

* * * *

J.P. stood at the drawing room window, looking out on the grey skies and just a light dusting of snow that touched the vegetation of Roscarrock Island. The sound of his siblings, nieces and nephews echoed around the walls of the ancient house, but he barely noticed, too busy thinking of Anne and all the many things she'd told him about her life. It was as if she'd wanted to tell him everything about herself, all at once. As if time ran out for them.

"I know I should pretend otherwise, but I cannot," she had confessed to him through a closed door. *"I do not want my adventure to be over."*

As if it were a matter of life and death that they have this adventure together.

Such a strange dream he'd had last night, of Anne telling her aunt and sister all about the first time he met her. It should have been a good dream, but instead it had left him with an unsettled spirit, and he woke in a cold sweat of anxiety. His stomach, even now, was in knots.

He heard footsteps and then the door behind him crashing open. "John Paul, there you are!" It was his father, with sand on his boots and a letter in one hand. He must have ridden to the mainland to fetch the post. "What the devil has been going on?"

J.P. turned slowly and set down his brandy glass. "What do you mean?" What was he being accused of now?

"You told your mother that you delivered Miss Follyot into her sister's care just outside the county."

He frowned. "Yes. I did."

True Deverell shook his head and held out his hand, the letter waving in his fingers. "This note from her aunt tells a different story. I suggest you explain yourself."

Utterly confounded, he took the letter and read quickly.

"...so I leave at once for London to be at her bedside. Perhaps you will explain to your son, on my behalf, why poor dear Anne was not there to meet him. The landlady said she must have run out into the alley to wait for his carriage and somehow, on the icy ground she slipped, falling in the path of the omnibus. The last thing she was heard to say was that she had not yet bought her rose madder silk, but no one can make sense of that for Anne was always a girl who preferred brown. She has not woken since, nor opened her eyes, but the physician says we must not give up hope. Anne is a strong young woman and stubborn. I am quite sure she is not yet ready to give up on life. My niece is far away now in her mind and her dreams, but if there is a way to come back to us, I am sure she will find it..."

His throat tightened; his head throbbed. "How can it—? She was there! I saw her, heard her, spoke to her." He'd kissed her too and there was nothing unreal about that.

"You're pale," his father exclaimed. "Good god, sit, before you fall down."

Too late. He had fallen already.

"*We shall fight off the undead together in this side of the house where they inevitably wander. I am not afraid of them and, in fact, feel some affinity with the lost souls caught between heaven and earth."*

She was not ready for her adventure to be over; she'd made that clear.

He'd missed her so many times. Again he saw himself tossing his hat into her fumbling hands as he stormed arrogantly across Mrs. Marvington's threshold for his Thursday visit. The moth hole in her bonnet ribbon had caught his eye.

She was there in his peripheral vision, but he didn't see her properly.

For months she'd worked in his shop, under his nose, and he'd not seen her.

If not for her trunk in the street, causing him to trip and fall, he would have missed her again. He would have gone to Mrs. Marvington's and never returned to the shop until late, thereby missing Shepherd and not seeing the letter asking him to escort Anne to her aunt.

The omnibus could have thwarted them yet again.

This time, Anne, somehow, had made sure it didn't. With stubborn determination and something even more powerful, she'd made certain she had her journey with him, after all.

"I just asked Jarvis," his father said. "He told me you got to the boarding house but the girl was already gone and nobody indoors would answer the bell so you drove on without her. I've not yet said anything to your mother. She's so happy to have you home. I don't want to spoil it for her."

"Father," he said, his voice sounding odd in his own ears, "you have to believe me. She was there. I know everything about her." He took a breath, the letter drifting from his fingers. "I saw her, finally."

"Were you drunk?"

"No!" He looked around, desperate to find an answer. And then, suddenly swept with calm, he said, "Father, will you take me to the train station? There's no time to waste, and I don't want to disturb Jarvis again, but I have to go back to London."

"Alright. But don't tell your mother. You know how she feels about steam engines and I don't want to get on her bad side. Not at Christmas." He faltered, a hand on his son's arm. "Are you sure, you're fit to travel? You look very ill. In fact you look as if you've seen a ghost."

He had. Like Ebenezer Scrooge, he'd been visited by the ghosts of Christmas past, present and future. And now he had a heroine to rescue. If it was not too late.

* * * *

London, New Year's Eve 1877

"She has made no sound or movement since they brought her in," the physician explained. "She was lucky the wheels of the omnibus did not run over her skull, but it was still knocked hard on the cobbles. There are a few broken bones, but they could be reset. The head injury is of most concern. If only we could get some reaction, but...alas..."

A petite lady with a tired smile sat by her bed, reading softly from a book, which she closed and put away when he came in.

"You must be Mr. John Paul Deverell," she said. "You won't remember me, for you were just a boy when you came to our vicarage."

"Oh, I remember, madam." He took her hand and kissed it. "Your niece reminded me."

She looked surprised. "Well, it is good of you to come and visit her." She put her head on one side. "Did you meet Anne recently? I thought you had not seen her since the vicarage party."

"I have met Anne many times. She and I are good friends. Very good friends."

"Really? She never said in any of her letters that she knew you."

"Well, let me see—I know that she is very fond of novels; that she was once swept down river in her little wooden cot during a flood; that she invented water-proof socks for her father, and that she would like to have studied veterinary science, if she were a boy." He smiled. "She is not afraid of ghosts or mice, was raised on her father's home-made wines, and likes to wrap gifts as much as she likes unwrapping them. I'm sure there is much more she wants to tell me, but our journey was interrupted." He looked around. "Is her sister here?"

"Yes, Lizzie— Mrs. Ingram— brought me here as soon as she learned what had happened."

And thus the letter was sent to J.P.'s mother and he would find out that Anne was not really there with him. The illusion— and the journey— was over and she had to let him go.

"Where is the snow angel?" he muttered

"Gracious! You know about that? Lizzie said her sister took it everywhere with her. We put it by the bed for her, but somebody must have taken it away. I came this morning to sit with her and it was gone. I shall ask the nurse when she comes in."

"That's alright," he said softly. "I think the snow angel looked after her long enough. It was only paper and the best I could do at the time." He walked to the bed and placed a wooden box on the blanket. "I bought her a new snow angel to look after her. One that will last a very, very long time." When he opened the ivory-inlaid lid, a pretty little doll, in white silk, feathers and glass beads, spun in circles to The Wexford Carol.

"What a lovely gift," said her aunt. "So very perfect for Anne. Her favorite carol too! How clever. I had no idea you and she were well acquainted. It is not like Anne to keep secrets."

"But this was a special one. You see—" He took Anne's limp hand in his. He swallowed hard. "We're going to be married. She meant to tell you when we got to Widecombe."

The lady gripped the back of her chair. "How extraordinary!"

"Yes." He smiled. "She is rather, isn't she? Not a woman to be overlooked."

"But Anne...Anne said she wasn't ready to marry. She wanted to be a modern girl."

"Oh, I know that too." He squeezed the hand he held. "It doesn't have to be tomorrow, or a year from now. Or fifty. Whenever she feels ready to be my wife. I will let her be whatever she wants. As long as I'm there with her, the snow angel can have all the adventures she desires." He leaned over and whispered, "I remember you, my darling Anne. I see you."

Her lashes fluttered. The corner or her mouth twitched.

The aunt, crying out in astonishment, ran to find the physician.

J.P. leaned over, kissed her lips, "And I love you, Anne Follyot. You're a remarkable woman and a menace. And I will love you forever. But you knew that already. You just had to find a way to show me."

That powerful thing with which she'd stolen away on his carriage and enchanted him completely? It was love.

When she opened her eyes and smiled, he knew more things too. More wonderful things that lifted his heart and made him take her in his arms.

Miracles could happen, especially at Christmas. Even to a man like him.

* * * *

1878
London

Anne finally bought her yards of rose madder silk and, with her Aunt Follyot's help, made for herself a very fine dress. Since the accident her sight was not as clear as it once was, her hand less steady, her speech uncertain, but she was as determined as ever to get what she wanted, and her perseverance astonished everybody. Except for J.P., who seemed to know exactly how strong-minded she could be when she set her mind to something, and so he never argued with her.

She didn't even have to tell him what she liked and wanted. They could sit for hours in silence and still enjoy each other's company. Apparently, they were very good friends, although she couldn't remember much about that at first. Not really. Little pieces of memory came back from time to time, and she wrote them down, fearing they might be lost again.

Anne did not mind that she couldn't remember everything about him, for she enjoyed herself immensely finding it all out again. Story by story.

He took her on many adventures, to the coast and the north, even abroad.

The good thing about having been run over by an omnibus was that folk felt great pity for her and she got away with a great deal that she probably shouldn't have. Including traveling about, unchaperoned, with Mr. J.P. Deverell. Certain folk in her family declared themselves shocked. Others thought there was no harm in it; after all, he took very good care of her and Anne was happy.

He had brought her back to life, as Aunt Follyot liked to say, so how could anybody argue against the two of them being together?

When Wilfred complained, "This modernity of yours, Anne, is going too far!" she replied, "I was struck down and killed by an omnibus, brother. I think I might be allowed the man of my choosing."

"Those two items having nothing to do with each other! And you were not killed, were you?"

"Indeed I was. For two entire minutes. And my return to life gave me a new appreciation for it. I don't mean to waste any more time."

You see, she could get away with all sorts of mischief now.

Eventually, she supposed, she'd have to marry J.P. To make an honest man of him. For now, she delighted in causing a little scandal every so often.

One evening, at a restaurant in London, he introduced her to a Lady Greville. He did not have to tell her that this woman was a former lover; the lady's expression of envy and sadness told her all that.

"We have not met before, have we?" Lady Greville asked, frowning faintly as she raised a closed fan to her chin. "Something about you seems familiar."

"No, your ladyship. I'm sure our paths would never have crossed."

"I suppose not." The woman sighed and looked her up and down, causing Anne to be very glad of her beautiful rose madder gown. "What a surprise you are. Not what I would have expected J.P. to fall in love with. But there you are. Men! So unpredictable."

"In love with me?" she exclaimed, looking askance.

"I told you I am," he muttered from the corner of his lips.

"Oh. I don't remember that."

He looked down at her, amusement shining in his lovely eyes. "Yes, you do. You just like me to keep saying it."

Incredible how he knew her so well. They must have always been very good friends for him to know everything about her. How lucky she was to have him.

She did not even have to tell J.P. how much she loved him in return. He knew it without a word being said.

"I know that you adore me," he'd say, smug. "You can't help yourself. It's all over your face, and you could never conceal anything from me. Never."

True. But Anne had an inkling that something else must have happened that made him so sure of her love that he never questioned it.

They moved into his house on Arlington Street, and every Christmas J.P. Deverell organized magnificent festive celebrations for all his employees at Lockreedy and Velder.

When Shepherd, newly promoted to the desk that once belonged to Jacob Dockery, reminded him that Christmas used to be his least favorite time of year, he replied only with a wink and a smile, content to keep his secret.

"Is it not odd," Anne remarked once, "that your beloved fiancée had to be struck down by an omnibus at Christmas to make you love the season?"

And he laughed, slipping an arm around her waist. "But I'm a Deverell. We do things differently."

He called her his miracle.

"You miss the point, my love. It is not that you were struck down by an omnibus, but that you survived and I saved you."

"You?" she cried. "You were not even there. You were late, which is why I ran out into the icy street to look for you. According to Mrs. Smith."

"But I had a hand in saving you. It was my handsome irresistibility that gave you the sheer will to live. You clung to life waiting for me to come back for you. I was your ghost of Christmas Future, and you were mine."

She laughed. "Are you sure I am the one with the injured head?" She reached up to touch his hair. "Perhaps 'tis you."

He turned his head and kissed her wrist. "My parts are all in sensible, excellent working order."

"Excellent, yes. Naughty, definitely. Sensible? Not necessarily."

He laughed, sweeping her up to carry her off to bed. His bed. Now hers too.

At night, she opened the wooden box he'd given her and watched the snow angel dance, glittering as the moon caught on her beaded halo. Often she drifted off to sleep watching the angel on her bedside table, wondering how she and a Deverell came into her life.

She was glad they both belonged to her. In time, her memories would return. She hoped she'd be able to talk clearly and see detail as she once did.

But she had a Deverell who loved her, and a girl really couldn't have everything, could she?

He was the best Christmas gift she ever had, and she unwrapped him every day.

Epilogue
1927

It was a peaceful house, well insulated with thick stone walls and a slate roof, cozily tucked away in its sheltered valley. Tonight, while the countryside around it slept under a counterpane of glistening snow, smoke puffed gracefully from its chimneys and inside the residents of the house went about their various Christmas Eve pleasures— slyly wrapping last-minute parcels, sneaking another chocolate from the box, sipping mulled wine and humming about partridges in pear trees. At the top of the house, in her bed beneath a dormer window, a young girl finally fell asleep.

Her great grandfather, carefully closed the lid over the snow angel and set her back on the shelf.

Such a long time ago and yet it could have been yesterday.

He got up, his bones creaking. Well, perhaps not yesterday.

Looking out of the window, he watched the snow falling. His weary gaze followed it downward, to the garden below. He squinted.

There, in the moonlight, a young woman danced, her arms out, her eyes laughing with pleasure.

Anne? He caught his breath. She spun in the snow, heedless of the cold.

She stopped, saw him watching, and waved for him to come out.

"Daft woman, you'll catch your death out there," he whispered.

But she was enjoying herself, leaping about, youthful again, her cheeks pink, long, dark curls loose about her shoulders.

His heart hurt with love, remembering every moment they'd shared.

* * * *

As he left the house, he heard their voices behind him.

"Was that the front door?"

"Yes. Your grandfather just went outside."

"What? It must be midnight, at least. What is he doing out there?"

"I don't know. I asked him where he was off to, but he didn't answer."

"For heaven's sake."

He heard the squeak of an angry palm rubbing a clear spot upon the kitchen window so that they could look out and watch him trudge across the snow in his slippers..

* * * *

"What are you doing out here all alone, woman?"

Anne turned to find him walking toward her through the moonlit snow. "I had to visit the past for a while." She beamed and tucked her arm under his. "I knew you'd join me."

"And what were you doing in the past?"

"I had to make sure I put that trunk in your way, didn't I?"

He scowled.

The handsomest man in the world and he was all hers. He shook snow from his black hair and those broad, firm shoulders.

"I had to make sure I tripped you up," she added. "Otherwise you would have missed me."

His brow smoothed, he laughed. "So that was you, was it?"

"Of course. Who else?"

"Come here and kiss me."

So she did. In each other's arms— in each other's eyes—they were young again, all their aches and pains swept away and as much in love as they had always been. It could all have happened yesterday.

Anne looked over at the house. "Our granddaughter is scowling at us from the kitchen window. We're about to get a lecture on not being twenty anymore, not being fit to dance outside in the snow at midnight."

"What do they know? They're children. They haven't lived yet."

"And it's Christmas." She kissed him passionately and he wound his arms around her, their strength holding her as they had for so many years.

"You're determined to cause a scandal, Anne Deverell. I think she just dropped a nutcracker."

"I suppose we'd better go inside then and stop misbehaving."

Arm in arm, laughing together about all those memories, real or imagined, they strolled back to the house, warm in each other's embrace and considering all the adventures they had yet to enjoy.

"I told the little one about the snow angel tonight," said J.P.

"Not all of it, I hope!"

"Oh no. It was the censored version. After all, it is Christmas."

"Yes." Sometimes, when Anne looked at her husband, she was not entirely certain that he had told her everything there was to tell about the snow angel and how she came into their lives. But he made up a good story. Almost as good as the ones she told.

Unfortunately she couldn't quite remember it all herself and had to rely on what he told her, however miraculous it seemed. However unlikely.

As they entered the hall and she turned to close the front door, Anne glanced up once more at the moon and smiled. She brushed snow from her shoulder and thought, just for a moment that she saw white feathers floating through the air.

Maybe, just maybe, it really was all true.

COMING SOON

The Snow Angel

Also from Jayne Fresina and TEP:

Souls Dryft

The Taming of the Tudor Male Series

Seducing the Beast

Once A Rogue

The Savage and the Stiff Upper Lip

The Deverells

True Story

Storm

Chasing Raven

Ransom Redeemed

Damon Undone

The Snow Angel

The Snow Angel

Pumpymuckles

Ladies Most Unlikely

The Trouble with His Lordship's Trousers

The Danger in Desperate Bonnets

The Bounce in the Captain's Boots

A Private Collection

Last Rake Standing

The Peculiar Folly of Long Legged Meg

The Peculiar Pink Toes of Lady Flora

The Mutinous Contemplations of Gemma Groot

Slowly Fell
Slowly Rising

Bespoke
COMING SOON

Jayne Fresina

ABOUT THE AUTHOR

Jayne Fresina sprouted up in England, the youngest in a family of four daughters. Entertained by her father's colorful tales of growing up in the countryside, and surrounded by opinionated sisters - all with far more exciting lives than hers - she's always had inspiration for her beleaguered heroes and unstoppable heroines.

Website at:
jaynefresinaromanceauthor.blogspot.com

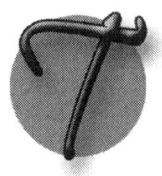

Twisted E Publishing, LLC
www.twistedepublishing.com

Made in the USA
San Bernardino, CA
11 January 2019